"LAST ONE," SHE SAID WITH A WRY SMILE, reaching for a chocolate truffle.

An idea struck him. Even though he questioned the wisdom of it, he couldn't resist. "Well, you should do something special since it's your last one for a week." He picked up the chocolate. "You should let me feed it to you."

Senada shook her head and shot him a skeptical glance. "Oh, no."

"Yeah, you should. It'll be memorable."

"No." She reached for it, but he moved his hand. They fought over it, her hand reaching and his quickly moving it aside. Finally the truffle was smushed.

"Sorry. You want something else?" he asked.

"No, I want that one."

He lifted his fingers to her mouth. "Then take it. . . ."

WHAT ARE *LOVESWEPT* ROMANCES?

They are stories of true romance and touching emotion. We believe those two very important ingredients are constants in our highly sensual and very believable stories in the LOVE-SWEPT line. Our goal is to give you, the reader, stories of consistently high quality that may sometimes make you laugh, sometimes make you cry, but are always fresh and creative and contain many delightful surprises within their pages.

Most romance fans read an enormous number of books. Those they truly love, they keep. Others may be traded with friends and soon forgotten. We hope that each LOVESWEPT romance will be a treasure—a "keeper." We will always try to publish

LOVE STORIES YOU'LL NEVER FORGET
BY AUTHORS YOU'LL ALWAYS REMEMBER

The Editors

Loveswept ®794

FOR THE LOVE OF SIN

LEANNE BANKS

BANTAM BOOKS
NEW YORK · TORONTO · LONDON · SYDNEY · AUCKLAND

FOR THE LOVE OF SIN

A Bantam Book / July 1996

LOVESWEPT *and the wave design are registered trademarks of*
Bantam Books, a division of Bantam Doubleday Dell Publishing Group,
Inc. Registered in U.S. Patent and Trademark Office and elsewhere.

ISBN 0-553-44505-7

Published simultaneously in the United States and Canada

Bantam Books are published by Bantam Books, a division of Bantam Dou-
bleday Dell Publishing Group, Inc. Its trademark, consisting of the words
"Bantam Books" and the portrayal of a rooster, is Registered in U.S. Patent
and Trademark Office and in other countries. Marca Registrada. Bantam
Books, 1540 Broadway, New York, New York 10036.

PRINTED IN THE UNITED STATES OF AMERICA
OPM   0 9 8 7 6 5 4 3 2 1

To Eric, for motivation and inspiration

Special acknowledgments to Donna
Beard and Karen Britton for sharing
technical knowledge and personal
experience

PROLOGUE

"I wish someone would go after her," Lisa Pendleton said, exasperation tugging at her features as she toyed with her food. "Someone who could *reason* with her."

Troy Pendleton took another bite of chicken and watched his brother Brick nearly choke on his iced tea. This was the first family meal his sister, brothers, and their assorted spouses and children had shared since Lisa gave birth to triplets.

"Reason?" Brick repeated to his wife. "When has anyone been able to reason with Senada Calhoun?"

Lisa scowled at him. "You just never understood her."

"Me and the rest of the human—" Brick muttered, then broke off and sighed. He drummed his fingers on the table. "Maybe Jarod—"

Jarod Pendleton shook his head. "I used my vacation for my honeymoon." He grinned and wrapped his arm around his new wife, Augusta.

Troy rolled his eyes at the lovesick couple and reached for another roll.

"One of Garth's mares just foaled," Jarod pointed out gently, eliminating another brother. "And Daniel's busiest season is starting now."

"That leaves . . ."

A long silence followed Lisa's statement. Troy paused while buttering his roll and looked up to find everyone staring at him. Worst of all, Lisa was looking at him as if he were the last great hope. Realization dawned. He immediately shook his head. "No way."

"I'm worried about her," Lisa said in earnest. "One day she was my business partner and friend, the next, she sold her share of the partnership and left for some bar in Texas."

"Maybe she needed a change." Lord knew, Troy felt like he needed one. His restlessness was eating him from the inside out.

"Something is wrong. I can feel it. I'd go after her if I could, but with the babies . . ." She lifted her hands helplessly.

Troy was tempted to offer to keep the kids in lieu of going after Senada Calhoun. His only obstacle was that he couldn't breastfeed. "You need someone who can reason with her. I sure as hell can't."

"I need someone who can find out what's wrong with her first," Lisa corrected.

Troy's interest in the elaborate home-cooked meal waned. He dropped the uneaten roll to his plate. "Senada and I don't get along." What man *could* get along with a woman whose nickname was Sin, a woman who seemed to take the greatest pleasure in tormenting a man with her blow-off-the-roof sensuality? A woman who, he was convinced, was a few sandwiches short of a picnic.

Lisa placed her hand on his arm. "Show a little compassion, Troy. I know you've got some in there somewhere."

Troy held his breath for a long moment. A glimmer of concern flickered to life inside him. Even for Senada, this behavior was unusual. What if there was something seriously wrong? What if she needed help? He snorted at the thought of Senada accepting help from him. Age-old self-protective instincts rushed to the surface, and he shook his head. "Give it up. There's nothing you can say that will make me go tearing after Senada Calhoun. Nothing."

When Lisa continued to look at him with that please-help-me expression on her face, Troy lifted his hands in exasperation. "I'd have to be certifiably crazy to go after her."

ONE

He was certifiable all right, Troy thought as he eyed the desert landscape with distaste. Someone should have tossed him into the loony bin and thrown away the key. Slamming his rental car door shut, he walked toward Padre's Saloon.

In the back of his mind, he hoped this little mercy mission would earn him enough respect from his brothers to give him more control over the family farm. Thus far, they'd wanted his brawn, not his brains, and the growing need to leave his own mark was making him restless.

Even so, he still wasn't quite sure how he'd allowed himself to get talked into this. All Troy knew was that he was there to get some answers, and he would do what it took to get them. He'd also been instructed to persuade Senada Calhoun to return to Chattanooga. That, he thought as he stepped into the busy watering hole, could get a little tricky.

Peanut shells littered the scarred wooden floor. Cowboy paraphernalia decorated the walls. His stomach growled at the scent of hamburgers and beer. Past the haze of cigarette smoke and what seemed like a herd of male bodies, he immediately spotted Senada.

Troy watched her give instructions to a waitress, then turn her attention to the customers, moving from one table to another. Her hair swung in a long black silky mantle past her shoulders, her eyes flashed with a hint of the fire in her personality, and her smile, well, her smile could tempt Saint Peter.

She probably thought the black jeans and frilly white shirt she wore covered enough to discourage male attention. Perhaps on another woman they would, but Senada's black jeans cupped and molded her hips the way a man would want to cup and mold her with his hands. Her blouse had a ribbon that held the white material against her tanned skin.

Troy bet every man in the place was rubbing his fingers together with an itch to tug that ribbon loose. In his own gut, he felt a visceral tension grab and clench.

Shaking his head, he put the first sensation down to temporary insanity and the second . . . to indigestion. He moved toward her, and by the time he got within talking distance, her back was facing him. He hesitated a second, feeling as if he were preparing to walk straight into a fire.

He shook off the ridiculous thought. "Any chance a guy from Tennessee can get a beer around here?"

Senada whirled around, her dark brown eyes wide with surprise.

There was something different about her, he noticed instantly. Her usual flirty demeanor was missing, and she didn't quite conceal a flash of vulnerability. Then he could almost swear he saw steam coming out of her ears.

Senada frowned. "Lisa sent you."

Troy shrugged. No use denying it.

"She shouldn't have."

"She was worried."

"There's no need. I'm fine. I—"

He grinned. "What am I gonna have to do to get that beer?"

Senada stopped and took a deep breath. She wanted to club him. Lord help her, the last thing she needed was one of the Pendleton brothers planting his size 12 feet into her life. "This way," she said tersely, and headed for the bar.

"Interesting place you've got here," Troy said.

"I don't own it. I manage it." She motioned for the bartender. "Rico, please give this man a beer."

"On the house?" Troy asked, needling her a

little to gauge her reaction, as he leaned against the bar.

Senada paused in the act of pouring herself a glass of water and looked at him sideways. "Consider it one for the road."

Troy laughed. Maybe this was the change he needed after all. He leaned closer, matching her haughty expression with a steady gaze. "Darlin', my return flight's not booked. I'm here for the duration."

Impatience gnawed at Senada, and she seriously considered throwing the water in his handsome face. It took all her effort, but she stifled the urge. "Then make the duration short. There's no need for you to stay on my account."

"There is a need." He took a long swallow of beer. "I need to know why you left Chattanooga, and—"

She pushed her hand through her hair. "I told you. I needed a change."

Troy shook his head in disbelief. "Here? You would deliberately choose to leave a thriving up-scale catering business for this?"

"My mother is from this area," Senada said, and took another sip of her water.

"Are you living with her?"

Senada didn't know why she felt compelled to answer his questions, except she knew that if she didn't give him some excuse, he would never leave her alone. "No, I'm not living with her."

"Is she sick?"

"No," she said quickly, feeling the familiar pinch of loss. "She's dead."

Troy paused a half beat. "When?"

"Years ago." She neither expected nor received sympathy from Troy. She knew the Pendletons had lost their mother and father, yet somehow they had come out stronger because of it. Until lately, she thought she'd become stronger because of her losses too. "Listen, I need to get back to work. There's no need for you to be—"

He caught her arm. "I need, because I made a promise. I can't leave here until I'm satisfied that you're okay."

The determined look in his violet eyes unnerved her. "It's really none of your business."

"It is now."

Senada took a calming breath. No need to get upset, she told herself. She could handle Troy. She'd always sensed she made him a little uncomfortable, a little off balance. She preferred it that way. Instead of pulling away, she stepped closer and smiled. "Why Troy, I would have never dreamed you cared. You're an intelligent man. Now take a good look," she dared him. "Can you honestly say I look like I'm suffering?"

She withstood his narrowed gaze and felt a measure of surprise that he focused on her face instead of her breasts.

He lightly traced beneath her eyes with his calloused thumb. "Dark circles?"

Another dart of surprise raced through her. He was more perceptive than she'd thought, and she would be looking for a new concealer tomorrow. "A good time and late night will catch up with the best of us," she lied with a shrug, and slipped away. "You should know that. Now you've done your brotherly duty. Give Lisa my best and tell her I'm fine."

Senada turned her back to him and wished with all her heart that she wasn't lying. Because she wasn't fine.

Troy watched her deliberately avoid him for the rest of the evening.

"Muy attractiva, si?" a man next to him said.

Unfortunately, the only Spanish Troy knew was what he'd learned from Speedy Gonzales cartoons and Terminator movies. "Pardon?"

The man snickered. "One hot woman, that Senada. Yes?"

"Yeah," he said, sizing up the man. "You know her well?"

"Not well enough." He gave Troy a meaningful glance. "She is a beautiful tease. All the men try, but she goes home alone. My name is Juan Marcheta. You are new?"

"Visiting from Tennessee. I'm Troy Pendleton."

"You do not sound like the Texans."

Troy chuckled. He supposed he sounded

pretty foreign to this guy. "I guess not. You know anywhere I can get a room for the night?"

Juan recommended a few places, then left Troy to ponder the puzzle of Senada. Although he would be the first to admit he had the sensitivity of a block of wood, he suspected something strange was going on. Aside from Senada's abrupt departure from Chattanooga, she usually had a half-dozen men dangling on her line. The fact that she wasn't seeing anyone gave him pause.

Women.

Troy shook his head. With the exception of Ethan and Nathan, his brothers had all lost their minds. They'd turned his existence upside down. They'd gotten married.

And now, because his sister-in-law was worried, he was in a two-bit Texas border town, and he was not only supposed to get some answers from a woman, he was supposed to reason with one—a crazy one at that.

He swore under his breath. This family duty stuff was for the birds, but Troy was a man of his word. Sliding back into the hard wooden chair, he ordered a burger and nursed another beer and watched Senada.

It was two A.M. when Senada pushed the key into the doorknob of her small but well-maintained rental home. Feeling a prickling sensation on the back of her neck, she stopped and turned around. Probably Juan, she thought, staring into the darkness. He'd followed her home another time.

"The answer is no," she said, wishing her porch light hadn't burned out.

Her heart sprinted when she saw the silhouette of a big male form. Juan wasn't that tall.

The moonlight hit Troy's face as he stepped forward. "I didn't ask." His mouth tilted. "Yet."

Relief sputtered through her, followed quickly by irritation. "What are you doing here?"

He shrugged and opened the door for her. "Just wanted to see where you live."

Senada kept her back to the doorway. "It would have been polite to warn me."

"It would have been polite for you to invite me," he corrected in a low voice, and met her gaze.

"It's late."

Troy nodded but didn't graciously back off. His blue eyes didn't waver, his jaw was set in a firm line.

She sighed and led the way into her living room. "Three minutes," she told him, and flicked on a lamp.

He shoved his hands in his pockets and prowled around the small room. "Looks like rental furniture."

She'd always known Troy was big, but having

him in her home made her more aware of the fact. Two minutes and thirty seconds, she noted. "Mine's in storage. This was quicker, easier."

"Why were you in such a hurry?" he asked, turning back to her.

Tossing her purse on the sofa, she shrugged. "I don't know. I needed a change. Haven't you ever felt like you needed to make a change and it had to be now?"

"Yeah, but moving halfway across the country requires a little planning," Troy drawled, stepping closer.

"For you," she conceded, and flipped her hair behind her shoulder. "I've been told I'm impulsive."

"Maybe." He gave her a long considering look, his gaze brushing over her body and returning to her face. "But there's more to the story, isn't there, Sin?" he said in a low voice.

It was an intimate, you-can-trust-me voice, and she felt the lick of temptation. She'd always thought Troy, with his six-foot-plus height, unapologetic chauvinism, and blatant masculinity, was a little over the top.

Too much had been her assessment. Too big. Too rugged. Too intractable. Senada had always been the one to hold the aces when it came to male/female relationships. She suspected Troy preferred calling the shots. They wouldn't mix well. Still, he was a strong man, more than physically strong, and that strength appealed to her now when she was vulnerable. Maybe he could handle the truth.

He cocked his head to one side and lifted his hand to cup her cheek. "Something *is* going on," he mused. "Tell me and I'll help."

Her heart tugged. His hand was gentle, his gaze warm. She'd locked herself away from human kindness over the last few weeks and suddenly felt the loss. It would only take one step, and she would be in his arms.

In that second, she thought of her big, strong father and how he'd been unable to handle the truth. She took a giant step back, physically and emotionally. "It's been three minutes."

"I'm gonna find out," he told her.

Sin shook her head and headed for the door. "You're wasting your time."

"I already know you're not seeing any men, and Lord knows that's out of character."

She whipped around. "How do you know that?"

"Juan, but I would have found out anyway." He twisted his lips in a cynical grin. "I'm the youngest of seven brothers, Sin. When you're the youngest, you learn by watching, so I'm damn good at watching. And just so you'll know, another characteristic about the youngest is that people underestimate you." His gaze fell over her like a hot brand, then he looked into her eyes. "Hasta la vista, baby."

❖━━━━━❖

Troy didn't like the accommodations.

His hotel room was the size of a closet, and if he turned over in his bed, he would land on the floor. No AC, no fan. To make matters worse, the walls were thin, and it sounded as if the guy next door had gotten very lucky tonight.

To distract himself from the explicit cries of his neighbors, he thought about Senada. More convinced than ever that something strange was going on, he considered the possibilities. She could be sick, but it didn't make sense that she would abandon her home and friends for that reason.

She could also be pregnant.

If the guy had dumped her, maybe she felt humiliated and didn't want to face her friends. He frowned. The only catch was that he'd never heard of anyone dumping Senada. She went through men like tissues and always appeared to be the one to move on.

He remembered how soft her cheek had felt in his palm, and the appealing mix of fire and vulnerability in her eyes. For a minute there, she'd looked as if she wanted to trust him, as if she would share her secrets with him.

He swore, kicking off the sheet. This was going to take patience, and he'd never been patient. He deliberately closed his eyes, and the image of her stole past the barrier in his mind.

Her mouth was red and taunting, her eyes, dark and sensual. His body heated. He swore again.

His dear beloved brothers had sent him straight to hell.

Over the following nights, Senada tried to ignore Troy. It should have been easy. Most of her customers were male. Many watched her, but none with Troy's unwavering intensity. He wasn't the least bit sly about it, just propped himself on a stool at the bar, nodded his head in greeting, and watched.

She really didn't need this, she thought, five days after he arrived. She'd fled to San Pedro with the intention of going to her father, but once she'd arrived, she chickened out.

If her father had been unable to handle her mother's illness thirteen years earlier, how could he deal with Senada's current crisis?

So, here she was, still shocked and afraid, and trying to adjust to a new and totally necessary lifestyle. She shook her head and checked the time. These days she was more conscious of the clock.

Juan sidled up to her. "This man from Tennessee. Troy. He comes every night. Is he bothering you?"

She flicked a glance at Troy and saw that he must have overheard. "Bothering me?" she repeated. *Yes.*

Another regular customer came up behind Juan. "Yeah, like stalking."

Senada wrinkled her eyebrows. "I don't know if I'd really call it stalking. It's more—"

Juan waved his friend up to the bar. "If he's bothering you, you should let us know and we'll take care of him."

Senada rolled her eyes. She could practically smell the machismo. "He's not doing—"

"We can make him go away."

She felt a stab of alarm. If this got out of hand, it could get messy, and Senada didn't consider breaking up fights one of the perks of her new job. "You don't need to do anything. He'll be going away very soon," she said, throwing a meaningful glance in Troy's direction.

Troy shook his head. "I'm not leaving until I get what I came for."

Juan stiffened and pointed his finger at Troy. "What makes you think you have rights over Senada?"

Pausing, Troy gave a warning glance at Juan's accusing finger. He took an unrushed swallow of beer and leaned back in his seat, clearly sure of his power. "Not that it's any of your business, but I've got rights with Senada."

Then he looked at Senada, and she felt the impact of his take-no-prisoners gaze to her toes. "She left me at the altar."

TWO

After being ignored for days, Troy felt a measure of satisfaction at seeing Senada stare at him in shock. "I may not be the only one she's left at the altar," he continued, elaborating on his fabrication, "but I think I deserve some answers. Wouldn't you?" He shot Juan a challenging glance. "She told me that all those stories about her ex-husband having to be—"

"Ex-husband!" Senada repeated, apparently finding her voice.

"—rushed to the hospital on their wedding night were just rumors."

"The hospital," she sputtered. "You're lying." She looked at Troy as if he'd lost his mind. "You're crazy. You're—"

Troy nodded. "That's right. Crazy for you. You stood with me at the altar, then left me. I deserve a chance to win her back." He nodded at the men. "Agreed?"

Juan looked uncertainly from Senada to Troy.

A waitress gave Senada a searching glance. "Why'd you dump him?"

"I didn't! He's lying. I never promised him anything. He's crazy. He just wants . . ." She took a breath, running out of words.

"He just wants what, señorita? Or is it, señora?" Juan added meaningfully.

"Can you honestly say you didn't stand beside me at the altar?" Troy demanded, recalling Lisa and Brick's wedding, where Senada had been a bridesmaid.

She paused, her eyes narrowing. "No, but that wasn't our—"

"There you have it, boys. From her very own mouth."

Juan motioned his friends backward. "A man deserves to claim his woman."

Senada slammed the pitcher of beer down on the counter. "His woman, my fanny."

"Appreciate your understanding," Troy interjected with a nod.

She glared at him with enough heat to melt iron, then seared him with a rush of Spanish words for which he could only guess the meaning.

She narrowed her eyes. "You know, up until this moment, you just annoyed me," she told him as she rounded the counter. "I had decided you were pushy because you were misguided. And if you were a little thick upstairs, it was probably just genetic, since the rest of your brothers seemed to be the same way. When people annoy me, I ignore them."

She leaned closer to him, and Troy was amazed at the quick leap of response in his body. "Now, I really don't like you," she whispered in a voice that shouldn't have been but was outrageously seductive. Her eyes were nearly black with emotion, and Troy felt himself sinking.

He closed his own eyes, blinking at the odd sensations inside him. Before he knew it, cold beer gushed down his head. Senada put the empty pitcher on the counter. He swore. His hair was drenched, his shirt wet. "What in hell—" He swore again, jerking away and shaking his head.

Senada smiled. "That's what I do to people I don't like. Don't mess with me, Pendleton. You are out of your league."

After his shower, Troy received a call from his brother Brick. "Nothing yet," he said, toweling dry his hair. "I knew she was moody, but you could have warned me about her temper."

"Lisa says she doesn't like being told what to do. And she gets really upset if she thinks someone is trying to put one over on her," Brick said.

Troy glanced at his beer-drenched shirt wadded up in the corner of his room and nodded. "Yeah, I figured that out."

"Well, if you screwed up, Lisa says Senada loves chocolate." Brick lowered his voice. "Personally, I'd recommend ducking. What do you think is wrong with her, anyway?"

"I don't know, but I'll find out. Even if it kills me," he muttered, then asked about the farm. After a couple of minutes, he finished his conversation and gazed around his new living quarters. A vast improvement over the hotel, the two-room garage apartment was still too small and hot, but it was clean. After sizing Troy up, his elderly landlord had given him a list of rules a mile long and required two month's rent in advance. But as they say in real estate, location is everything. His present location was perfect for his purpose.

Before, his determination to solve the mystery of Sin had been a matter of his promise to his brother and sister-in-law. Now, male pride and a near self-destructive determination drove him. He pushed the curtains aside and looked out his window. Two doors down and across the street stood Senada's house. He could just imagine her delight when she learned who her new neighbor was.

❖ ━━━ ❖

The finger prick still hurt, Senada thought as she tested her blood. She just wasn't very good at sticking herself. She jotted down the date, time, and results in the little notebook, then eyed the syringe warily.

"The needle is my friend," she told herself.

"Liar," she whispered back, and started to perspire. Her anxiety was strictly related to that damn needle, not her lack of insulin. She took a breath and grabbed a premoistened alcohol pad.

"Right thigh, today," she said, wishing her voice had a more soothing effect on her nerves. She brushed the pad over her thigh, then poised the syringe over the same area.

"The needle is my friend." Her overriding instinct was to close her eyes, but she'd learned it hurt worse when she missed her targeted area. "This is not my leg." Denial worked for the millisecond she needed, and Senada plunged the syringe into her thigh.

She swore at the sharp sting. "That was most definitely my leg." Her hands trembling, she tossed the used syringe away and stood. It should be easier now, she thought, glancing at her watch. But it wasn't. She kept waiting for the day when she didn't mind living by the clock, making sure she ate every four hours, testing her blood, and giving her own injections of insulin. But Senada had always lived by her own clock and her own rules, so she was furious that her body had betrayed her.

There should be a rule somewhere that people who were afraid of needles didn't develop insulin-dependent diabetes. There should be another rule that chocoholics didn't develop diabetes. There should be, but there wasn't.

As much as she would like to ignore the intrusion of her recent diagnosis, Senada couldn't. She knew her mother had died of complications from diabetes. Either from ignorance or neglect, her mother hadn't been conscientious about her health. Senada had inherited her mother's height, her expressive brown eyes, and thick, black hair. Unfortunately, she'd also inherited the diabetes.

The doctors assured her, however, that she could live a long, healthy life if she took care of herself. She'd been careless about that area in the past. Her idea of taking care of herself had been luxuriating in a bubble bath and sleeping until noon on her day off every now and then.

A healthy diet was a necessity now. A regular schedule was a given. She stretched her shoulders against the sudden sensation of being tied down. The needles and the lack of chocolate were tough to endure, but the most difficult for her so far was the loss of freedom.

She sighed and made a face at the mirror. After extensive negotiations with her dietician, they had found a way for her to have a chocolate dessert once a week. And tonight was the night for her devil's food cupcake filled with chocolate cream.

Senada brushed her hair from her face and smiled wryly. Meat, vegetables, and a small portion of grains first, but then the cupcake. "Better than sex," she murmured in sweet anticipation.

Forty-five minutes later, she'd lit a candle, put soft music on to play in the background, and had eaten her vegetables. She removed her empty plate from the table.

The moment had arrived. Her heart beat faster. Her mouth began to water. Taking a deep breath, she stripped off the cellophane wrapper. It had been over a month.

The doorbell rang.

Senada sighed, giving a backward glance toward the door. She contemplated quickly biting the top off of the cupcake, but was determined not to rush this rare, small pleasure. She left the table and pulled open the door to Troy Pendleton.

She tried to close it, but his big foot prevented her.

"C'mon, Sin, give me a break. I'm here to apologize."

That gave her pause.

"Sort of," he added.

She gave the door another push.

"I brought chocolates."

She opened the door and stared. "Chocolates?"

He gave a slow grin as if he'd just shot two through a basketball hoop. It was a grin designed to get past a woman's defenses. Other women, she thought, would find that grin appealing. "You mentioned an apology?" she prompted, noting the box of candy.

"Are you going to invite me in?" He looked past her.

No. "I'm a little busy right now. I—" She broke off when she spotted her neighbor, Mrs. Rodriguez, running toward them at a breakneck pace. Senada had met a few of her neighbors, but Mrs. Rodriguez had been the most welcoming. The effusive, nurturing woman had even brought her homemade bread.

"My husband! My husband! He is dead!" Then she tore into a flurry of Spanish.

Senada shared a look of alarm with Troy, and all three rushed to the Rodriguez's house. At first glance, Mr. Rodriguez did look dead, sitting limply in his chair with his head propped back and his mouth open. But Troy quickly determined the man was breathing. In the back of her mind, she noticed and appreciated Troy's quick, calm manner. While Senada comforted her neighbor and called for an ambulance, Troy located a bottle behind the chair.

Apparently, the man had mixed alcohol with his medication. He would need medical attention but would be okay. By the time the ambulance arrived, Mr. Rodriguez was awake but groggy. Senada and Troy left while Mrs. Rodriguez read her husband the riot act in Spanish.

"I appreciate your help," she told him as he followed her inside her house. Her antipathy toward Troy had faded. How could she hate him when he'd allowed Mrs. Rodriguez to blubber all over him?

"For a minute there, I didn't know who was going to need medical treatment more, Mrs. Rodriguez or her husband."

Senada grinned. "She's very emotional." She glanced at the table. The candle was gutted and the music had stopped. The lone cupcake, however, remained.

She shook her head. "Well, this has been an exciting evening."

Troy nodded. "Yeah, I'm starvin'." He picked up her cupcake. "You don't mind, do you?"

Senada watched in horror as he took a bite. "Wait!"

He paused, glancing at her, then the cupcake. "It's okay," he assured her. "A little stale, but nothing's wrong with it."

Senada bit back a whimper. She'd only bought one cupcake because she couldn't stand the temptation of having several around the house.

Troy swallowed another bite. "I apologize

about the conversation with Juan, but I had to get him off my back." He didn't like explaining himself but had concluded it was necessary if he didn't want any more beer dumped on his head. "And this way, I figured I could get him to leave you alone too. Sort of kill two birds with one stone." He took another bite and polished off the cupcake.

He glanced at Senada. She was wearing a strange expression. If he didn't know better, he would swear she was going to cry. "Something wrong?"

She stared at the empty paper cupcake liner. "Sin?"

Her gaze met his. "I want my cupcake back."

Troy blinked. "Your cupcake?"

She nodded. "I want it back. I've waited over four weeks to eat that cupcake, and I want it back."

"Four weeks," he echoed. "It wasn't that stale."

"I want my cupcake."

Troy shot her a wary glance. The woman was loony. She must be on some strange kind of diet that was affecting her brain, he thought, then assessed her curves with masculine appreciation. "You don't need to be on a diet. Why don't you eat some of the chocolate candy I brought you?"

She hesitated, then sighed. "Let me see them."

Troy lifted the lid off the box and presented them to her.

Senada closed her eyes and drew in a deep breath. She looked as if she were having an erotic experience. "They smell wonderful," she whispered.

The sensual expression on her face tugged at something inside him. Her whisper heated his skin. He pulled at his collar.

She carefully selected three pieces of candy and set them on a napkin in front of her. He expected her to put one whole piece in her mouth at a time. Instead, she took a small bite of the first chocolate and rolled it around in her mouth. He could practically imagine her tongue working over the morsel.

He watched her throat ripple when she swallowed.

"I know this makes no sense to you, but it's been over a month since I've had chocolate, so I'm not reasonable about it."

He watched her lick a chocolate buttercream center, and his gut tightened. He cleared his throat. "Lisa mentioned you have a, uh, weakness for chocolate."

"She wasn't lying." Sin took another tiny bite and closed her eyes. "I can give up a lot of things, but this one's tough."

"Then why deprive yourself?" He was feeling a little deprived just watching her.

She shrugged. "Necessity." She picked up the second piece. "And this has got to last a week."

Troy watched, mesmerized, as she sucked the cherry from the center. His body grew warm at the sight of her pink tongue skimming over her lips. If her mouth did that to a little piece of chocolate, then what would she do to a man? He stifled a groan at the intimate image.

"You mind if I get some water?" he asked. When she absently shook her head, he headed for the refrigerator. Her attention was fixed on the chocolate with such intensity that he wondered if the rumors about her past lovers being carted off to the hospital were true. Troy pressed the cold glass to his forehead, then took a quick gulp.

Senada glanced up at him. "Could I have just a sip of that?"

"Sure." He set the glass in front of her and watched her drink. He swallowed when she swallowed.

She gave him a wry smile. "Last one."

Troy nodded. "You want me to light the candle for you?"

She sighed. "No."

Her eyelids fluttered downward, and an insane idea struck him. He went with it even though he questioned the wisdom of it. "Well, you should do something special since it's your last one for a week."

She glanced up. "Think so?"

"Yeah." He picked up the last chocolate. "You should let me feed it to you."

Senada shook her head and shot him a skeptical glance. "Oh no."

"Yeah, you should. It'll be memorable."

"No." She reached for the chocolate, but he moved his hand.

"Yeah."

"No," she said more forcefully, reaching again.

Troy zigged. She zagged. And the truffle was smushed.

She looked at him in disgust. "You smashed my truffle."

"Sorry about that."

"You ate my cupcake."

He nodded. "You want another one?"

"No I want that one. That truffle."

He lifted his fingers to her mouth. "Then take it."

"I should get a knife," she said, frowning at him.

"I don't think I trust you with a knife," he said, wary of the gleam in her gaze.

Senada rolled her eyes. "Okay, I'm not wasting that truffle." She pulled his hand closer and looked at him again. "I hope you're enjoying this." Then she took her first lick.

Troy felt the sensation of her kitten-soft tongue in every erogenous zone of his body. It was a bizarre form of torture, watching Senada Calhoun lick chocolate from his fingers.

He never would have suspected his fingers were sensitive. He never would have suspected he could become completely and totally aroused by such a simple action of a woman's mouth on his finger. Especially when that woman didn't even like him. But her spicy scent combined with the bittersweet smell of chocolate and liquor made him take short, shallow breaths because he feared intoxication.

Her single-minded attention and overtly expressed pleasure made him sweat. Her exotic eyes were hooded as if she were overcome with desire. Her full lips pouted as if she'd been kissed and wanted more. When her tongue skimmed the inside of his middle finger, it was all he could do not to groan.

Still holding his hand, she gave him a considering glance. "You know, if I bit, it would really hurt."

He met her gaze and tried to hide his arousal. "Maybe," he conceded, not bothering to keep the dare from his voice.

She gave a double take and looked at him again. This time, Troy knew she was considering him sexually. Her dark eyelashes swept down, shielding her eyes the same way a filmy nightgown shielded a woman's body. A gentle tease. He wondered if she knew how that affected a man. How it affected him.

She gently put his hand away from her. "That was a delicious truffle, even though you smashed it. Maybe even better than the cupcake," she said with a slight, smoky smile. "And it was certainly memorable. Thank you for the chocolates."

Standing, she gave a little shrug. "Guess you'd better head back to your hotel. You'll want an early check-out so you can get back to Tennessee."

Troy shook his head. He was going to kill his brothers for this detail. K-i-l-l them. He willed his body to forget what it was hoping for, then he stood. "As a matter of fact, I've already checked out of the hotel."

Senada's face lit up with delight. "Well, be sure to tell Lisa I said hello. I'll give her a call sometime. I promise. I just have to settle some things here first and—"

"What kind of things?" he interjected, allowing her to lead him to the door.

She gave a vague gesture with her hand. "Oh, things." She opened the door.

Troy slipped his arm around her waist and pointed to his new domicile. "You see that house down there."

She glanced at him with furrowed eyebrows. "Yes."

"You see the garage apartment?"

Her eyes glinted with suspicion. "Yes."

"If you need anything, day or night," he told
her, "I'll be there." He thought about kissing
her, but based on her hostile expression, he
thought she really might bite him this time.
"Anytime, Sin. Night or day."

THREE

Senada's dietician got a kick out of the chocolate cupcake story. In retrospect, Senada even found it amusing.

"This is the first time I've seen you laugh since you've been here," Helen Waverly said. "Maybe Troy Pendleton isn't all bad."

"Maybe not," she murmured. "But he's bad enough." Her feelings about Troy were constantly changing. When he informed her that he lived two doors down from her, she could have cheerfully dumped another pitcher of beer on him. When he helped her with her neighbor, she'd almost liked him. And when he fed her the chocolate truffle, she'd felt a surprising shot of sexual attraction. Very surprising. Since her diagnosis she'd felt frozen, at least as far as her femininity was concerned.

Now she didn't. Senada wasn't sure she liked the source of the change.

"Have you called your father yet?" Helen asked.

"Not yet. I'm still trying to decide *how* to do it."

Helen arched her eyebrow at the excuse but let it pass. "And have you thought about attending a meeting of the local support group?"

Senada shifted. "I'm thinking about that too."

"You can't stay in a holding pattern forever," she said gently.

Senada nodded. "I know." She deliberately changed the subject. "But about those chocolates?"

Helen rolled her eyes. "Put them in the freezer. They'll last longer that way. *One* a day," she said, lifting her index finger for emphasis, "with a meal."

Senada smiled. "You don't know how happy you've made me."

They had a full house on Friday evening, and Senada was busier than ever. Several customers casually asked her about Troy. She acted as if she didn't know what they were talking about, but the back of her neck prickled with irritation. In the short time that he'd been there, he'd made a place for himself. The men greeted him; the waitresses flirted with him. At this very moment, he was in the back because the cook had asked him to take a look at the ice maker.

"Here you go," she said, placing two pitchers of beer and four frosty mugs on a table. She shot a quick glance at the men dressed in denims and sporting cowboy hats. "Welcome to Padre's. Are you new to town? I haven't seen you before."

One man gave her a long considering look. "We're from the Circle K. I'm Chris Grant, the foreman."

Circle K. Her father's ranch. The room began to swim. Senada blinked, then took a careful breath and smiled. "Bet that job keeps you busy. I hear it's a pretty big operation."

He shrugged. "Busy enough, but Calhoun lets me off to come into town every now and then. Maybe I could show you the spread sometime. What's your name?"

Senada paused. She considered conjuring up an alias and immediately felt impatient with her cowardice. So what if her father learned she was there. Maybe it was time. "Senada," she said, and gave the group of men a half grin as she left. "If you need anything, yell."

Her mind spinning, she slapped the door to the back room so hard, it hit the wall as she rushed through it.

Straight into Troy.

"Whoa!" He grabbed her shoulders.

"Sorry," she muttered, still shaken.

He frowned, studying her. "What's wrong? You look like somebody hit you."

"Nobody hit me," she told him. "Not really."

He cocked his head to one side. "Hit *on* you?"

The tray she held separated her chest from his, but his hands felt warm and reassuring. His gaze was strong but gentle, and the combination sent a tumbling sensation in her stomach. For a moment, she considered dropping the tray and putting her arms around him.

She shook her head and immediately backed away. *Where did that thought come from?* She rolled her eyes. "They all order beer, and they all hit on me. It's part of the program." She looked past him. "What have you done to my ice maker?"

"Fixed it." He pushed her hair behind one shoulder. "How are you gonna compensate me?"

He touched her as if it were no big deal, and it shouldn't have been, but Senada felt her heart race. She swallowed an oath. Maybe she needed to check her blood sugar. "Your beer's on the house. I'll even throw in a burger if you want."

"You're all heart," he said wryly.

"That's me, sweet as—"

"—Tabasco sauce."

She flicked her gaze back up to him. "Go home."

He gave a slow, terrible, wicked grin and leaned close to her. "Not until I get what I came for."

"Troy," she said, throwing his innuendo right back, "you wouldn't know what to do with it once you got it."

Troy's eyes lit with challenge, and he leaned dangerously close.

"You little thief!" The cook's voice rang out. "What are you doing with those hamburgers? Six of them. I oughta—"

Senada broke away and rounded the corner to find a little boy, terrified and defiant, holding burgers in his hands. "It was only five! Pig!" he yelled back at the cook. "You're a stupid pig!"

Pete's face turned purple. "Why, you little—"

Senada's heart twisted. "Hold on, Pete," she said to the cook, then quickly assessed the boy. His clothes were worn, his cheek was smeared with dirt, and he wasn't wearing any shoes. "Are you hungry?"

The boy jutted out his chin. "So what if I am?"

She walked closer. "For starters, you could ask before taking the burgers. How old are you, anyway?"

"Twelve."

"More like nine," Troy muttered from behind her. "You gonna eat all those yourself?"

The kid looked at Troy warily, clearly intimi-
dated by his size. "Maybe. What's it to you?"

Troy shrugged and leaned against the
counter. "Nothing. Go ahead. I'd just hate to
see you get sick."

"Sick?"

"Five burgers is a lot to eat."

"It was six," Pete insisted. "Six of my
burgers."

"I'll cover it," Senada said, finding the situation disturbing. "You can cook some more."

Pete grumbled as he made his way to the
refrigerator.

"I wasn't gonna eat them all," the boy said.

Troy nodded. "You got a name?"

"Rocky."

"You got a family?"

Rocky's brown eyes glittered with defiance
again. "Yeah. So what?"

"Where do you live?"

The boy made a quick dash for the door, but
Troy was quicker. He caught the boy by the arm.

"Lemme go!"

"Where do you live?"

Rocky glared at Troy. "We ain't got no
house. It's my mom, my sister, and me. My dad's
in jail. My mom cleans rooms at the hotel, and
we ain't got no house."

It hit Senada hard. She couldn't exactly say

why. Maybe she was still reeling from meeting someone from her father's ranch. Maybe Helen's words about how she should get involved with other people had finally taken hold. Either way, Senada felt as if someone had hit her in the stomach. *Wake up. Things could be worse. There are other people in this world in far worse circumstances than yours.*

Her eyes met Troy's, and the steadiness of his gaze calmed her. She cleared her throat. "You didn't say where you live," she finally said very quietly.

Rocky lifted his thin shoulders. "For the last two weeks we've slept in a warehouse."

Troy took a deep breath. He knew what he was going to have to do. "How would you like a real roof over your head for a change?"

"I don't want social services."

Troy gave a wry laugh. "Do I look like social services? I have access to a two-bedroom garage apartment. You think your mom would like that?"

"Maybe."

"Yeah, well, how about I walk with you to your mom's, and we can ask her."

"Can I keep the burgers?"

Senada blinked, spurred into action. "Yes. Just a minute, and I'll give you some soda." She filled some cups, gave them to Troy. "And here are some nachos. If you want more," she told

Rocky, "let me know, and I'll get them for you. Okay?"

"Okay," the boy said in a surprised voice. "Thanks."

Senada looked at Troy curiously. "This sounds like your apartment. You're ready to go back to Tennessee?"

Troy wasn't certain he heard hope or disappointment in her voice. "No chance, Sin. I'm headed back to that crappy hotel." No AC. No fan. Stifling a groan, he paused. "Unless you'd like to show a little compassion and hospitality and let me stay with—"

"Sorry, no," she managed quicker than lightning, but Troy would have sworn she found it tough to refuse him.

He chuckled. The woman was begging him to leave at every turn. Her eyes, however, seemed to be begging for something else. He was obviously suffering from delusions. "Had to try. I'll see ya later, Sin. Lisa sent some baby pictures and told me to show them to you."

All wide eyes and tousled hair, she clasped her hands tightly together. "Okay."

Troy narrowed his eyes. She'd looked upset earlier, and she didn't look any happier now. Knowing she couldn't care less about his sleeping arrangements, he deliberately misunderstood her concern. "Hey," he said, chucking her gently under the chin, "don't worry about me.

It's a terrible motel and there's no air conditioner and I'm lonely, but I'll be okay."

She rolled her eyes and swatted at his hand. "You know, it's almost what you deserve. Are you sure you don't have a split personality? It amazes me how a complete jerk could do something so, so—" she glanced at Rocky, then back at Troy, "nice."

Troy grinned. "Just a backwater country boy keeping you on your toes."

After Troy got the Horge family settled in to *his* apartment and tossed most of his belongings in the backseat of his car, he noticed Senada's light was still on. Reluctant to face the hot little motel room that was waiting for him, he rang her doorbell.

He heard footsteps, followed by a long pause. She was probably trying to decide whether to open the door or not. He mugged for the peephole.

The door whisked open, and Senada stood there in a long silky-looking white robe holding a bowl of cereal. At that moment, he coveted both the body beneath the robe . . . and the cereal. His stomach growled.

"Hello to you too," she said.

"Noticed your light was still on," he said, edging forward.

She looked at him and sighed. "Rocky's family all moved into your apartment?"

"Yeah, and I didn't ever get those burgers you promised. It's hell being a hero."

Senada sighed again and held the door open with her shoulder. "Okay, come on in. Rice cereal or frosted corn flakes?"

"Both," he said, walking through the doorway toward the dining room. "Just give me the box. I'll eat the cardboard."

She chuckled and poured a big bowl combining both cereals, then added milk. "Here. What's Rocky's mother's name? I thought I'd take a bag of groceries over tomorrow."

"Maria, and she'd really appreciate it. They've got a few things to tide them over. Stuff I bought a few days ago." Glancing at Senada, he recalled his conversation earlier that day with Lisa and fished the photos out of his shirt pocket. "Take a look at the triplets. I swear, those babies change every day."

Senada reached for the pictures and smiled. "They're adorable. Oh, and Lisa cut her hair." She squinted her eyes. "Is Brick losing his?"

Troy laughed. "No, that's just a shadow, but I'll pass on your observation to him. I'm sure he'll appreciate it."

She met his gaze and arched her eyebrow. "He never liked me."

"I wouldn't say that."

She shot him a look of disbelief.

"More terror that you were going to find someone for Lisa before he could get his stuff together."

"He almost lost her."

"Yeah, but look at 'em now."

Senada sat in the chair next to him and shook her head. "It's hard for me to imagine having a family like yours. I don't think I could handle it. Do you ever feel stifled?"

Troy thought about that as he crunched his cereal. "Every once in a while, but we've had to hang together during some tough times." He glanced at her and wondered about the pensive expression on her face. "What about your family?"

"We're a lot more independent. My mother died when I was pretty young, and my father and I aren't close."

"So what do you do at Christmas?"

She tossed him a chiding look. "I'm not alone unless I want to be."

He'd bet she wasn't. Troy allowed his gaze to fall over her again. Her breasts made his hands itch to touch them, her waist was small, her hips slim but well curved. And her legs, well, he thought, looking at the bare tanned limbs, her legs were designed to shred a man's restraint. But it wasn't so much the physical package that set Sin apart from other women. It was her attitude. She was the most natural, unselfconsciously sexy woman he'd ever met.

Taking another bite, he shook off his useless thoughts. "I can't even begin to comprehend a holiday without too much food, too many kids, and an argument over who gets the last piece of pie."

She grinned at him. "And since you were the youngest brother, I bet you didn't get that last piece of pie very often."

"Until lately," he conceded, then switched the subject back to a troubling thought. "I know you're as independent as they come, but don't you *ever* wish you had someone to unload on?"

A lost expression flickered across her face, quickly replaced by a trace of irritation. She stood and took both their bowls to the sink. "It's all about what you learn. You learned to depend. I learned not to."

He followed her to the kitchen. "Sounds like a complete lack of supervision. I can just imagine what kind of trouble you got into when you were a teenager. Now, if you'd been a Pendleton, we would have locked you in your—"

She turned around and tilted her head, her brown eyes meeting his. "But I'm not a Pendleton. What are you after, Troy?"

"Answers." Damp from her shower, her hair left a dark spot on the shoulder of her robe. He'd waited just about as long as he'd wanted to to touch her, so he lifted a strand of her hair. Slippery as satin, like her robe.

Her gaze assessed him. "And that's all, right?"

He didn't let go of her hair, and he didn't back off from her gaze. "I've been told I have the sensitivity of a block of wood."

Senada bit her lip to stifle a chuckle. "I can see that."

"I've been told that I don't know when to stop." He slipped his broad fingers through her hair to the back of her head.

Senada let him. Later, she would have to figure out why. "I can agree with that," she murmured. She still thought he was going overboard, but he really had the most incredible violet eyes.

"And I've been told I'm brutally honest." He deliberately looked at her mouth, then back at her eyes. "It wasn't meant as a compliment."

She resisted the urge to lick her lips but couldn't produce a quick retort.

"I'm gonna be brutally honest right now. You make me curious, Senada. Sometimes I wonder if you're a witch. Sometimes I'm sure you're just a scared little girl in a woman's body."

Senada flinched. That last observation was too close for comfort. "I'm not—"

He lowered his head, blocking out the light and cutting off her protest. "Seems like the more I learn about you . . ." He skimmed his mouth against her lips in a taunting movement, and she felt his thighs brush against hers as he stepped closer. "The more I want to know."

His hand cupped the small of her back. He drew her body flush against his and took her mouth.

She stiffened, expecting him to rush, to plunder her mouth. His hands were firm, but his lips were gentle, seeking, asking, wanting.

Her heart tripped in surprise.

He was everything she hadn't anticipated. He massaged her nape with his calloused hand at the same time he flicked his tongue on the seam of her lips. Soothing and arousing her.

A slow, insidious hunger wound its way through her. She instinctively parted her lips and waited for him to explore her mouth, but he didn't. Instead, he suckled her bottom lip between his.

His gentleness was at odds with the hard ridge of his masculinity pressing against her. He squeezed her in his arms and gave a low growl. "God, you taste like heaven and hell."

He slipped his hand up her ribcage to just below her breast. Senada's heart pounded. She wanted . . . his touch. She lifted her hands and slipped her fingers through his hair. He ran his tongue just inside her lips, his fingertips grazing the underside of her breast.

Her chest hurt to breathe. She wanted more. But still he played with her, his fingers edging close to her nipple then scooting away, his tongue dipping inside her mouth then darting back. Her blood was burning her. Her breasts were aching with arousal.

He slipped his finger close again, toyed with her tongue again. Her frustration shot through the roof. "Kiss me," she whispered against his mouth. "Really kiss me."

FOUR

"That's what I'm doing" he murmured, and his fingertips moved terribly, wonderfully closer.

"No, you're not," she managed. "You're playing with me."

Troy continued to sip at her lips. "Don't wanna rush."

Senada groaned and took matters into her own hands. She rubbed her aching breasts against his chest in search of relief. Slipping her tongue past his lips, she began her own exploration.

Troy gave an answering moan and covered her breast with his palm. He slid his other hand through the fold of her robe, and when his fingers encountered the bare flesh of her bottom, he broke off and swore. "You're not wearing a damn thing underneath that." His hand still cupping her, he sucked in a deep breath of air. "Not a damn thing." Senada blinked and clung to his shoulders. The kiss had just been getting good. Why had he stopped? "I just took a shower. What am I supposed to be wearing?" She arched against him and took his mouth again.

She felt his chest expand against hers as he let her take her fill. His hand massaged her rear end, and he lifted her so that his denim-clad hardness fit between the notch of her thighs. Her head was spinning. Her heart was racing. She reveled in the sensations of arousal. It had been so long since she felt this alive, this feminine, this hungry.

His fingers slipped between her thighs and brushed her moistened femininity, and her arousal turned to undiluted need. She shimmied against his erection, and he shuddered.

Pulling back again, he took a deep breath and shook his head. "I'm going to take you on the dining room table, if we don't stop."

The room seemed to dip and sway. She stared at him, struggling to focus.

"And I'm not going to do you on the dining room table," he told her and swore. "Not until I spend at least twenty-four hours with you in bed."

Caught between overwhelming need and heady arousal, Senada didn't want to stop. For a few mind-blowing moments, he'd given her blessed amnesia. For a few moments, she'd forgotten her diabetes. And she wanted to keep on forgetting. She swayed toward him again, pressing her open mouth against his.

"Sin," he muttered, his voice heavy with need, aching with an undertone of protest. His tongue melded with hers. "We've got to stop." Slipping his tongue deeply in her mouth, he shuddered.

He gripped her shoulders and tore his mouth from hers. "Stop."

Frustration shot through her and she met his gaze. "Why?"

He looked at her as if she'd lost her mind. "Because we're out of control."

"So?" She knew she wasn't behaving rationally, but she hadn't felt so normal, no, better than normal, in what seemed like forever.

He pushed his hand through his hair and shook his head. "Are you saying you want to finish?" He gestured toward the table. "On the table? On the floor?"

"Yes," she said defiantly. Then reality began to filter through her brain. Did she really want to get into it with Troy Pendleton? "Well," she amended, looking at his hand on his belt. "I did."

Troy narrowed his eyes at her. "You wanna tell me what's going on, here?"

Her insides were trembling. She tightened the belt on her robe and looked away. "No need for a cross-examination. You were right. We were out of control. No big deal."

"No big deal?" He stood in front of her. "You tell me to go back to Tennessee every chance you get, then I kiss you, and you want to go all the way."

"Okay, so maybe you're better than I thought you would be," she said, appealing to his ego.

"Maybe," he said, "but something else is going on here. You seemed almost desperate."

Senada laughed out of sheer panic. "Oh, I think that's a bit much, Troy. I may have been turned on, but it's been a long time since I've been desperate."

She took a careful breath and strode toward the front door. "It doesn't really matter now, because the moment," she said, opening the door for him to leave, "has definitely passed."

Troy followed but stopped at the door and put his finger under her chin to study her face.

It was disconcerting, having his violet eyes trained on her, but she made herself withstand it. Senada decided Troy Pendleton was smarter than she'd thought. He had the potential to affect her in a way she hadn't planned. Even now, his unwavering gaze shook her. The intensity wasn't purely sexual, there was a deep element of human concern. It was easy for Senada to identify because it was so rare.

"It's time for you to leave," she whispered.

He dipped his head and pressed his lips to her forehead. "I'll be around."

Senada watched him go, then pushed the door closed and sank back against it. *Don't be fooled*, she told her pounding heart.

"I baked you and your nice Troy Pendleton a chocolate tortilla pie," Mrs. Rodriguez said in her lilting voice. She beamed as she presented Senada with the dessert.

"It looks delicious," Sin said, her mouth watering. She wondered what she could trade for just one piece of the decadent pastry.

"You will invite him for dessert and tell him I say thank you, *sí*?"

"I'll be sure to tell him," Sin said. "Let me put this in the refrigerator. I was just on my way out the door to take something over to the new neighbors."

"New neighbors?" Mrs. Rodriguez repeated. "I know nothing of new neighbors."

Senada smiled at the woman's indignant tone. She considered herself the official welcome representative for the neighborhood. "A mother and two children. She's had a rough time."

Mrs. Rodriguez clucked sympathetically. "Poor dears. You must let me come with you."

Senada gathered the food and shook her head. The poor dears would be adopted by Mrs. Rodriguez within five minutes. Not a bad thing, she thought. Not bad at all.

Mrs. Rodriguez chattered as she and Senada

walked to the garage apartment. Maria Horge, a petite dark-haired woman with shadows in her eyes, opened the door. She looked young to have two children. Young and defeated.

Senada's heart twisted. She smiled gently. "You must be Maria. I'm Senada Calhoun and this is—"

"I'm Hazel Rodriguez. We're your new neighbors, and we want to welcome you. Oh!" she exclaimed when she saw the two children, who were sitting at the kitchen bar eating cereal. "What beautiful children. What are their names?"

Rocky scowled, but his younger sister smiled.

Maria gave a faint smile too. "Rocky is my little man. He's nine. And Angel is five," she said, squeezing the little girl's shoulder. "You're so kind to come visit us, but the food—" She shook her head self-consciously. "You really shouldn't."

"It's not much," Senada assured her, and set the baked chicken and bread on the counter. She glanced at Mrs. Rodriguez as she moved closer to the kids. "Just a little neighborhood tradition. Here's my phone number," she said, pulling out an index card with the information written on it. "If you need something, call."

Maria seemed to be holding her breath.

Senada gazed at her thoughtfully. "Are you okay?"

"Everyone's so nice. Troy, you, Mrs. Rodriguez."

Senada laughed and tried to put her at ease. "No, no, no. We're just nosey neighbors. You'll see. Hope your kids like chicken."

"They love chicken," Maria assured her as a knock sounded at the back door. "Oh, look! It's Troy!"

Senada's gaze met Troy's, and she felt a ridiculous spurt of excitement. He looked as if he hadn't slept well, probably a by-product of where he'd spent the night. She wished she had a good reason for why she hadn't slept well.

"Good morning," he said, shifting the grocery bag he carried but keeping his eyes on her. "How are you?"

There was a hint of sexual turbulence in his gaze that caused an answering rumble inside her. Sin ignored it and smiled. "Fine. I was just on my way out the door." She deliberately looked at Maria. "It was nice meeting you. Do give me a call if you need me. Okay?"

She managed to get out the door before Troy could add anything. "Bye," she called, and cursed the breathless sensation in her chest. No good reason for it, she told herself. No good reason at all. Troy Pendleton was not her type.

Senada was still repeating the mantra twenty minutes later when he showed up on her doorstep.

"You have something for me," he said.

Senada blinked. "That was last night, and since then, I've come to my sen—"

"I'm talking about Mrs. Rodriguez's pie," Troy said dryly, and walked past her.

"Oh," she said, and fought the urge to kick herself. She quickly went to the refrigerator and pulled out the pie. Giving the chocolate pastry a wistful glance, she made a quick decision. "Here." She thrust the pie in his hands. "You can have the whole thing. Take it back to the hotel with you."

Troy looked at her as if she were crazy and pressed his hand to her forehead. "Are you sick? Or nuts?"

Impatience licked through her. "Neither. Just take the pie. Okay?"

"But you love chocolate."

"I'm turning over a new leaf," she told him. "I'm curbing some of my basic hungers."

"Well, don't do it on my account." He gave her a once-over and shoved his hands in his pockets. "Listen, there's nowhere I can put this in that shack where I'm staying. Do you mind if I eat it here?"

He looked rumpled, his violet eyes were a little cloudy, and there was a distinct razor cut on his chin. Past her mile-high defenses, Senada knew she had softened toward him for giving his apartment to Rocky and his family. "Sure," she said quietly. "Have a seat."

Troy did a double take. He hadn't heard her

use that tone of voice before. Soft, he thought, even her expression was soft. He sat in a chair and just stared at her.

She cut a piece of pie and set it in front of him, then lifted her finger to his chin. "Have an argument with your razor?"

"Dull. It's been a helluva morning. I talked to Brick."

"Problems?"

"The worst," he said, shaking his head. "Ethan eloped."

Senada frowned, clearly confused. "Did he marry a terrible woman?"

"Don't know," Troy said with a shrug. "Doesn't really matter. All I know is when one of my brothers elopes, it brings another woman into the family, and I get stuck with crazy assignments. And it doesn't matter which brother it is, whenever they get married, they start acting loopy."

Senada bit her lip in amusement.

Troy watched her. He could look at her full mouth for an hour, he thought, but he'd probably end up hard as a rock with no relief in sight. He forced himself to look at the pie.

"So you don't really think marriage is a good idea."

"I think men who get married and kamikaze pilots have a lot in common. It's called a death wish."

"My, my," she said, briefly sliding her hand

over his shoulder as she stood. "Some women might take that as a challenge to change your mind. Aren't you glad I'm not one of them?"

He took a quick look at her backside as she walked to the refrigerator, and shook his head. He didn't want Senada messing with his brain, but he sure as hell wouldn't mind her working on his body. In fact, his body had bemoaned the fact that he stopped her the night before. "I think I'm safe as long as the local Ladies' Club doesn't go after me."

"I wouldn't count on it."

"Why?" he said, watching her curiously as she poured a glass of water for herself and him.

"Well, I'm sure you know you have your attractions."

"No," he denied, taking a bite.

"Yes, you do," she said mildly. "Great body, killer eyes, nice smile when you get around to it. . . ."

"Sensitive as a brick, impatient, and tight."

"Tight," she echoed with a smile, sliding her gaze down to his rear end. "I thought I'd already covered your body."

The heat in her gaze made his throat clench around the bite of pie. He coughed. "Tight," he corrected, "as in cheap."

"You weren't cheap about giving up your apartment."

He shrugged, uncomfortable. "That's different."

"Yeah," she said, her tone full of disbelief. "The waitresses say you give good tips."

"No big deal."

"Uh-huh. *And* you bought me those expensive chocolates."

Troy resisted the urge to tug at his collar. Damn, it was hot. "I had to try to get back in your good graces. Futile endeavor."

She shook her head and her face grew incredibly, wonderfully closer to his. "Face it, Troy," she said in a whisper that held just a hint of bite. "You're one of the good guys. I can spot them a mile away. The Ladies' Club will eventually have you for breakfast."

Too tempting to resist. He caught her hair in his hand and tugged her mouth close to his. "Honey, you have no idea how good I am. Be glad to show you sometime. You might want to keep in mind I like it slow, but I can be fast."

He took her mouth. She tasted sweet and forbidden, with a touch of resistance that challenged and seduced. He swept his tongue past her full lips into her warm, moist mouth. There was nothing submissive about Sin, even her kiss. At the same time, he was conquering her mouth, she was conquering his.

She sucked his tongue into her mouth, and he felt the caress all the way to his groin. Tilting her head, she ran her tongue around his lips again and again until he was searching for breath. Then, she pulled away.

Just a little breathless herself, she tried to cover with a smile. "What a combination. Good guy and forbidden chocolate. Two reasons for me to stay away from you."

He snagged her hand. "When are you going to tell me why you really came down here?"

A shadow crossed over her eyes. "You're not going to find what you're looking for."

There was something important behind all this. He felt it in his gut. "Then I guess I'll just have to keep looking."

Senada downshifted as she drew closer to the sign for the Circle K Ranch. Looking down the driveway that had once led to her home, she felt her heart tighten in her chest. She pulled her little Miata to a stop on the side of the road and reeled from a wave of memories.

When her father first bought the ranch, the drive had been dirt. Now it was paved and the sign was flashier. She peered into the distance and saw a gate at the end of the lane. "My, my," she murmured to herself. "Dear old dad has done well after all."

Of course, she wouldn't be in a position to know since she hadn't spoken to him in seven years. He'd paid for her college education and attempted to send money for Christmas and her birthdays, but she'd just sent it back. Now, they didn't even exchange greeting cards.

She'd never forgiven him for walking out on her mother that last year before she died. He'd only made the situation worse when he brought Senada to live with him while he went through mistresses like tissue paper. She'd rocked his world when she was a rebellious teenager. He hadn't liked her makeup, her clothes, or her mouth. There'd rarely been a peaceable moment, and when she left for college, she'd left for good.

Senada glanced down at the sleeveless white shirtwaist dress she'd put on. Conservative, classy, Rex Calhoun would approve. After all these years, she still struggled with the absence of his love and approval.

She barely noticed the on and off traffic on the road until the black Mercedes convertible pulled into the lane. A young-looking blond woman with sunglasses drove past Sin.

Another mistress, she thought, and a hard knot formed in her stomach. A still harder resentment rose inside her. Rex might be richer, but he hadn't changed. Shaking her head, she put her car into gear and pulled back onto the road. She just wasn't ready to face her father yet.

She would kill him, Troy thought, if she knew he was following her. But hell, the woman didn't give him much choice. He could get more information out of a clam. He narrowed his eyes at the Circle K sign and wondered why she'd sat there staring down the lane so long. He wondered what the significance of the ranch was. He'd ask around at the bar tonight.

Troy eyed the speedometer and shook his head. Sin had a lead foot. Now why didn't that surprise him? Keeping one car between his rental sedan and her sports car, he followed her until she turned into a parking lot. He rounded the block, noted the building's occupant, and felt his stomach take a dip. Medical office. Could be a regular checkup, he told himself, but his gut wouldn't let him believe it.

He waited over an hour, then trailed her to a pharmacy. Fifteen minutes later, she came out with prescription bags.

He wiped his hand over his face, thinking his sister-in-law might not be thrilled with his update, so he decided to wait until he had more information. Either way, Senada Calhoun was full of secrets, and he was closer to finding out just what they were.

"I'll take that table," Senada said to the busy waitress and walked over to where Chris Grant was sitting. She was curious. "What can I get for you?" she asked him.

"Beer all around, and some 'skins.'" He looked her over. "Seems pretty busy. How ya doin' tonight?"

"Busy is good," she said with a smile. "How are things at the Circle K? Rex Calhoun driving you hard?"

"Yeah, the guy didn't turn that property around by sitting on his duff. He keeps his hands on the business end, but he likes riding with the guys every now and then." He grinned. "Of course, his lady takes up some of his time too."

"New girlfriend?" she asked, barely needing to hear his response.

"Nah." He shook his head. "His wife. She roped him about three years ago."

Senada just stared at him. The room was spinning. "Wife?" she echoed after a long moment. "You said his *wife*?"

"Yeah."

She blinked at him.

He laughed. "You look surprised. You weren't planning on going after the old man, were you?"

"I hardly think so," she thought, since she was the old man's *daughter*.

"Yeah, you're not really his type. He goes for—"

"Blondes," she finished for him, because Senada was quite familiar with her father's taste in women. "I'll get your order."

"Hey," he called after her. "Just cause you're not his type doesn't mean you're not mine."

She was so angry, she could barely see straight. It wasn't rational, it wasn't logical, but the heat flaring through her bloodstream would power a geyser. Senada took a deep breath to see past the red mist rising before her eyes and stretched her lips into a flirtatious smile. "I'll keep that in mind," she said, then headed for the kitchen.

Juan stepped in front of her. "When you going to give your man a second chance?"

His words were slurred, she noticed. "How many have you had tonight?"

"I dunno," he said with a shrug. "Been a rough week."

Senada counted to ten, then moved around him. Troy shifted away from the bar and walked beside her. "Problems?" he asked.

"Nothing major." She tossed her hair behind her shoulder. "Need to find out who's been serving Juan. I think he's reached his limit."

"Tonya," he said, watching her try to conceal the fire in her eyes. "Want me to tell her?"

"That would be nice."

"You look like you're ready to chew glass," he told her.

"Not so," she murmured, baring her teeth in a smile that would terrify most men. "I'd just like to break something."

A shout rang out behind them, and both Troy and Senada whipped around to see what was the matter. A middle-aged man was screaming in Spanish at Juan. The name Nita came up several times.

Senada sighed and headed toward the two men. "One of those nights."

Resisting the notion of Senada getting between two angry men, Troy held up his hand. "No. Give me a minute with 'em."

He walked toward the men. "Excuse me," he said, but both men ignored him. The middle-aged man was still going a mile a minute, and Troy, unfortunately, didn't have a clue what he was saying. The man finally ended by shoving Juan.

Juan said, "*Sí.*"

The other man threw one punch, then another. Troy stepped forward and took the next one on the cheek.

"Troy!" he distantly heard Senada call.

Troy shook off the pain. Swearing, he pushed the man backward until he was pinned against the wall. "Nita," was all the man said brokenly. "Nita."

Juan came up beside Troy and swiped at his bloodied nose. "It's okay. You can let him hit me. I got his daughter pregnant."

Troy swore again. "Outside. We're taking this outside." He pointed toward the door.

Senada appeared at his side. "Are you okay?"

"Yeah, let me get this taken care of." Troy wrinkled his cheek and winced. He was going to have one helluva bruise.

"You need some ice?" she persisted.

"Maybe later."

"You should have let me handle it."

Troy tossed her a dark look. "The bruise'll look better on me."

Twenty minutes later, he'd negotiated his way through a convoluted discussion in Spanish spat out accusingly by Nita's father and translated by an inebriated Juan. When he was certain no one was going to get killed, Troy sent both men home. By the time he returned to the bar, his cheek was throbbing. Tonya gave him beer, an ice bag, and a look of sympathy.

In a darkened corner, Troy slumped in a chair wondering what had possessed his brothers to send him down there. Why was he staying? If he wasn't taking abuse from Senada, he was asking for it from her customers, and suffering from lack of sleep in that horrible motel. Any man in his right mind would chuck it all and leave.

Troy glanced up at the sound of Senada laughing with a cowboy customer. Sin was flirting. No newsflash there.

The cowboy was kissing her hand. And Troy, who had never had a jealous moment in his life, wanted to rip the guy's lips off.

FIVE

An hour later, all the customers were gone and it was closing time. Senada bent down and peered at Troy's swollen cheek. Wincing, she put the ice bag back on. "You look terrible."

"Thanks," he said dryly, still irritated with his feelings of jealousy but lapping up every second of her undivided attention.

She frowned and pushed his hair back from his forehead. "You should have let me handle it."

"We already discussed that." The woman had wonderful hands, he thought, wonderful. "I didn't want you to get in the middle of that. You might get hurt."

She blinked at him. "Protective? Is this the infamous Pendleton protective streak?"

"Not really," he said with a shrug. "Logical move. I'm bigger than you are."

"But I understand Spanish."

"I don't like the idea of you on the floor."

Her lips twitched. "Pendleton protective-ness. I can't remember the last time a man was protective of me. What a novelty."

"Glad I brightened your day," Troy said in a dark tone.

Senada giggled. "Oh, and believe me, you did."

"Who were the friendly cowboys in the back?"

Her smile faded and her gaze slid from his. "Just some guys from the Circle K. They like to flirt."

"Uh-huh. The Circle K a big cattle ranch?" He watched her closely.

She stroked his hair back again. Her scent seemed to permeate his pores. The touch of her hand was distracting. She was distracting.

"Yeah, I hear it's pretty big." She cleared her throat. "I hear the owner just got married." Her eyes narrowed, then she seemed to shake off her pensive mood. "The foreman from the Circle K said the ranch is holding a big barbecue. He invited me to come."

Troy felt another surge of something ugly in his blood. "Is that so?"

"Yes." She gave him a considering look, and it was as if something clicked between them. "Wanna go with me?"

Fighting a rush of pure pleasure, he paused. "When?"

"I think it's next weekend," she said. "Of course, you might not still be in town."

The dare in her voice dug into his nerve endings. "I'll still be in town, and I'll go with you."

"You're acting like someone died," Senada said to Troy as they walked through the housewares department at the local store.

"Might as well be dead. He got married, didn't he?" Troy still thought it was sad that Ethan had lost his mind and plunged himself into the drowning sea of matrimony.

She turned away from the silver tea service to face him. "I think you need to rework your attitude about this, Troy. How many of your brothers are married now?"

He shook his head. "All except Nathan and me."

"What about your sister?"

"Carly was the first to go." He rubbed his chin. "Russ isn't a bad brother-in-law though."

"But your sisters-in-law are bad, mean-tempered shrews. Right?"

"Hell no," he said. "The women aren't that bad. It's just what they've done to my brothers."

"Are you saying your brothers are unhappy?"

Troy thought about that. "Not unhappy.

Just—" He searched for the right description. "Just nuts. Garth won't let Erin out of his sight for two minutes. He fusses over her every time she gets on one of their horses." He sighed and made a face. "Daniel and Sara make baby talk with each other. God, it's disgusting."

"And Brick?"

"Brick's the worst. He'll do *anything* Lisa asks him to do."

"Sounds like they're all in love."

"Yeah," he said glumly.

"And they're all happy about it." She nudged him. "Adjust. I bet Ethan's happy too."

"Brick said he sounded like a different man."

"So let's pick out the wedding gift. Isn't that why you asked me along? Do you know anything about his wife?"

"I think she's a little younger. She was a student at the university where he teaches."

"So they might not have all the necessities," she said, looking around. "Do you want to send crystal or something more practical?"

Troy took a deep breath of Senada's perfume. Damn, the woman even smelled like sin.

She looked at him as if she was expecting an answer.

Troy shrugged. "I don't know."

Twenty minutes later, they left with four crystal wine glasses and an electric ice cream maker. Senada led him into her house, and he immediately headed for the sofa. Since he'd been staying at the motel, creature comforts were few and far between. "Don't suppose you'd rent out this sofa?" he asked, slumping into the cushions.

"Sorry," she said with a laugh, and gave him a glass of lemonade. "You take up too much room."

"Discrimination," he muttered, and took a long cool drink.

"I-uh need to go do something in the back. Can you amuse yourself for a few minutes?"

"Sure." He looked at her, noticing the way she twisted her hands. "Anything wrong?"

"Oh, no," she said. But her voice was high. "Everything's fine. You just stay right here." She walked a few steps away. "And I'll be back in a few minutes."

Troy stared after her and shrugged. "Okay." She was a strange and wonderful woman, he thought. More strange than wonderful. He took advantage of the quiet to lie down on the sofa and close his eyes. The air was cool, the sofa soft. The room smelled clean. He drifted off. It seemed only seconds passed before a shriek jerked him awake.

Adrenaline pumping through him, Troy jumped to his feet and bolted down the hall. "Sin!" He quickly glanced through one bedroom door, then another. The bathroom door was closed. "Sin, are you okay?"

A lengthy silence passed.

He stepped closer to the door and tapped. "Sin?"

"I'm fine," she finally said. "Just dropped something. I'll be out in a minute. Sorry."

Troy shook his head. "Dropped something," he repeated, bemused. He put his hand on the doorknob. "Are you sure?"

"Yes. I'm okay. That little yell just popped out." She paused a half beat. "Go back to the living room," she told him in a voice that mixed nerves and amusement.

"Okay," he said, frowning and turning back down the hall. *Little yell?* He was surprised the neighbors weren't beating down the door. Hesitating at the end of the hallway, he turned and leaned against the wall.

Senada appeared from the bathroom. She glanced up, saw Troy, and closed the door behind her at the same time she gave him a big smile. "Hi there."

"You okay?"

She walked toward him. "Well, how do I look?" She ran her hand down his arm.

He fought the distraction. "You look like trouble."

Her eyes gleamed with mischief. "Who, me?"

"Yeah, you." He nodded down the hall. "Mind if I use your bathroom?"

Her smile vanished and her eyes rounded.

"I—uh—just a minute. I left it a mess this morning." She whipped away from him.

Troy lifted his hand in protest, but she'd already disappeared again. Within a minute, she popped back out with a bucket she toted toward her bedroom. "All yours," she called.

Walking into the pale pink bathroom, Troy glanced around, wondering what had made Senada scream. He closed the door and saw her silk robe on the hook. Cosmetics and perfume lined a shelf. The flowery bath curtain was pulled closed. He peeked past it into the tub. He knew he was being nosey, and felt a little guilty about it. Swearing, he took care of his business and washed his hands. Just as he was about to leave the bathroom, he spotted a wrapper beside the trash can. Bending down to pick it up, he read the label. Syringe.

Needles. Why would Sin need a medical syringe? His heart clenched in his chest. "What's she doing with needles?" No good reasons came to mind. He thought of the visit to the clinic and the pharmacy.

Senada Calhoun was full of secrets, and he was one step closer to uncovering one. He just wasn't sure he was going to like what he learned. He strolled back down the hall and shoved his hands in his pockets.

"Sorry to have to kick you out," she said, glancing at the clock, "but I've got to get to work."

"Okay," he said reluctantly. He had too many unanswered questions. "Thanks for helping me pick out a present for Ethan."

"No problem. I was born to shop."

"Yeah." He walked closer to her and looked at her. "Tell me something, Sin. Are you okay? Healthwise?"

"Why?" Suspicion narrowed her eyes for a second, then she flitted toward the front door. "Believe me, Troy," she said. "My lifestyle is healthier than it's ever been."

Healthier by choice or necessity? he wondered, but he sensed he didn't have a chance in hell of getting a straight answer to that one. Especially with her standing there holding the door open, waiting for him to leave. He walked past her and barely brushed his mouth over hers. "See ya in a little bit, Sin."

When Troy got in his car, he swore under his breath. He didn't like what he didn't know about Sin, but he did like that softly stunned look on her face after he'd kissed her.

Senada took a break after her third lap to catch her breath. Lord, how she hated exercise. Her dietician had insisted it was time for her to begin a regular exercise program. "An essential part of your health maintenance." Senada had chosen swimming because that way, at least, she wouldn't sweat. She'd forgotten, however, how tiring it was after even a few laps.

"Didn't know you swam."

Senada looked up past a pair of big feet, muscular calves, powerful thighs, dark blue swim trunks that didn't conceal the bulge of his masculinity, to a washboard flat abdomen. At that point, Sin closed her eyes and sank down into the cool water up to her neck.

Enough was enough.

"I just started. What a surprise meeting you here," she said in complete irony. It was obvious Troy had started following her. She just wasn't sure how long he'd been doing it.

"Yep." He jumped in beside her. "Great idea for getting away from the heat and out of that sorry excuse for a motel."

Senada fought a smile. "It's been very difficult for you to adjust to the high temperatures since you've been down here, hasn't it, Troy? Bet you'd give just about anything for a cool Tennessee breeze, wouldn't you?"

He sighed. "Yeah. Just about anything."

"So," she said, infusing her next words with all her persuasion, "why don't you go back to Beulah County for a little visit?"

He popped her with a little splash of water. Senada glared at him, trying not to admire his well-developed chest and incredibly broad shoulders.

"I can't go home until my mission here is

accomplished," he said in a wooing voice, and wrapped her in his violet gaze.

Senada sighed. It really was a shame she couldn't just regard him as an object of lust.

He put his hands on her shoulders and his gaze narrowed. "Since you're not helping me, God knows when that will be. Besides, I wouldn't dare give up the privilege of escorting you to the Circle K Barbecue."

Senada ignored the burning sensation where his hands touched her bare skin. She shrugged away from him. "You know, Troy, I like you a lot better when you don't talk so much."

Then she put her face in the water and swam.

Troy watched her, wishing he could see past those sexy brown eyes and read the truth beyond her flirty manner. Maybe if he held her long enough and kissed the easy lies from her lips, maybe if he made her body burn like she made his burn, the need for deceit would turn to ashes. Maybe if he laid himself bare, she would feel safe enough to drop her own facade, and Troy could see the real Senada.

He'd seen flashes of her before, flashes that tempted and taunted as much as her curvy body and catch-me-if-you-can manner. Flashes of a woman who touched him deep inside. The notion shocked him even though he'd realized it before.

Troy didn't want to be touched by a woman.

If the experience was anything like what he'd observed in his brothers, he'd end up *touched* in the head. Worse than that, though, Senada wasn't exactly the girl next door. He wondered if he laid himself bare for her, if she'd use him the way the rest had. Watching her swim toward him, he took a deep breath of fortitude. Come hell or high water, he was determined to come out of this mercy mission unscathed. He glanced at the water and grimaced. He had the high water right now. He'd been through hell. Heaven knew what was next.

"Nice quiet night," Troy said with satisfaction to Senada as she worked the bar.

"So far," she told him, tilting her head toward Juan. "He's been putting them back pretty fast."

A man stomped into the room and headed straight for Juan.

Senada winced. "Oh no. Not again. Mr. Salderos." She lifted a hand when Troy stood. "I'm handling it this time."

Mr. Salderos immediately started in on Juan. Senada caught all of the man's virulent words. He was clearly still upset about his unwed daughter's pregnancy.

Troy came to her side. "What's he saying?"

"He's calling Juan a slew of insulting names for getting his daughter pregnant and abandoning her." She turned to the man. "Mr. Salderos, I think it would be best—"

Mr. Salderos continued unabated.

Senada raised her voice. "*Silencio!*"

Mr. Salderos paused and stared at her, then turned to Juan and lifted his fist. Everything blurred together. Troy swore and pushed her away. Mr. Salderos's fist connected with Troy's mouth. Within a minute, all three men and Senada were outside in the dark parking lot.

Troy wiped his bloody mouth and winced. "We're not doing this again." He waved his hand at Senada. "You translate."

Troy pointed his finger at Mr. Salderos. "You are not coming in here again to start anything with Juan."

Senada repeated his words in Spanish.

"The next time, I'm hitting you back, and I'm not just hitting you once. I'm beginning to feel like I owe you." He glanced at Juan. "Both of you."

Senada translated for Mr. Salderos, and the older man backed slightly away.

Juan shrugged. "I deserve it. Let him hit me. She is the sweetest girl in the world, and I got her pregnant."

"If she's so damn sweet, why don't you just marry her?" Troy retorted, dabbing at his still-bleeding lip with the back of his hand.

"I would marry her, but her father won't let me see her."

Troy and Senada stared at each other.

"Translate, please," Troy said.

Senada repeated Juan's words to Mr. Salderos, and the old man looked at Juan in surprise.

"You wish to marry her?" he asked in Spanish.

"*Sí*," Juan said.

Mr. Salderos started talking again, this time in a brighter tone.

Troy regarded him with suspicion. "What's he saying? I'm not gonna have to hit him, am I?"

Senada shook her head. "He's setting the date for the wedding. Watch. They'll shake hands in a minute."

Sure enough. Three more minutes, and Mr. Salderos and Juan looked as if they could have been long-lost pals. Mr. Salderos patted Juan on the back and offered to take him home.

Senada glanced at Troy and took his hand in hers. "Let's go back in and get some ice for your lip."

"This is getting to be a habit," he grumbled, lacing his fingers more securely through hers. He liked the sensation of her inner palm nestled against his. For such an innocent gesture, it had a big impact on him.

"Think it says something about your arbitration skills?"

He pulled her to a stop just inside the door. "I didn't conduct the negotiations this time. I just stepped in when Mr. Salderos started to lose it."

She blinked. "You're right." Her voice softened and she touched his jaw. "Thank you."

Troy stood completely still. There was a rumbling deep inside him, and it wasn't for food. It was like the threat of an earthquake, shifting his foundations. He took a deep breath.

Her eyelashes drifted over her eyes, shielding her expression from him as she moved away. "I'll get you some ice. It's almost closing time, anyway. Go have a seat."

Senada gave Troy the ice, then avoided him for the next thirty minutes. She felt him watching her every move. Something about his gaze made her knees feel like jelly. Add to that the way he'd protected her, and she felt her defenses falling like a house of cards. Concentrating on the little tasks required to close the bar, she regained a little of her calm before she checked on him again.

"Let me see," she said, bending to check his lip. She winced. The bruise on his cheek was just now starting to fade. Troy's lip, however, was swollen. It looked painful. "I'm sorry," she said, shaking her head. She took the ice from his hand and held it against his mouth. "If you were at home, would Carly take care of this?"

"Probably," he muttered, his eyes intent, almost devouring.

Senada took a careful breath and fought a

rush of want. "What would she do? Fuss at you?" she asked, her voice breathless to her own ears.

"Fuss a little," he said, tugging her closer and spreading his legs open so she could step between them. "Then she'd probably say I need to find someone to kiss and make it better."

Senada was acutely aware of his masculine heat and scent. "I can't kiss your mouth," she whispered. "It would hurt you."

He pulled her down on his lap.

She could have pulled away, should have pulled away, but she wasn't remotely interested in going anywhere. Her chest felt tight, her heart was thumping, her nerve endings were jazzed. All because this man looked at her as if he'd like to eat her for dessert.

"Find somewhere else to kiss me, Sin."

SIX

Sin considered her options. She could tell him to forget it and leave, but there was a delicious fire in her blood and an irresistible I-dare-you glint in his violet eyes that made her want to play.

"Somewhere else," she repeated in mock despair as she brushed his hair off his forehead. "But there are too many choices." She leaned forward.

"I suppose," she continued, "I could kiss your forehead." She barely skimmed her lips over his forehead and felt him go very still. A heady sense of power swirled inside her.

"Or one of your eyelids." She gave a butterfly kiss on one of his eyelids.

"Or your cheek." She kissed the bruised one very gently but didn't move away. Instead she inhaled his scent. She liked the way he smelled, a unique blend of man and aftershave. She liked the sense of his strength beneath her. She liked feeling in control.

Troy wrapped one of his hands around her hips and drew her against the cradle of his hard masculinity. Her feeling of control flipped like a pancake. "Don't stop now," he said in a dark voice full of longing.

Something inside her tore a little. Restraint, denial frayed around the edges. The waitresses had gone. The cook had gone. Senada was acutely aware that they were alone.

It was more dark than light. She leaned forward and rubbed her open mouth just below his ear.

He sucked in a deep breath. "Touch me," he whispered.

Part plea, part demand, his words were intimate. Her heart thudded against her rib cage. "Where?"

"Anywhere," he murmured, moving his hands up her arms. "Everywhere."

So she kissed her reservations good-bye and kissed Troy Pendleton's neck instead. Bolder than she should have been, she unbuttoned his shirt and ran her hands over his artfully carved pectorals, skimming her fingernail over one nipple.

He shuddered.

"Want me to stop?" she asked.

"No," he growled, tugging at her shirt.

Senada licked his throat.

He swore, and within seconds, his hands cupped her breasts. His thumbs drew mesmerizing circles around her nipples.

Wicked sensations shot through her. "Oh!"

"Want me to stop?" he muttered.

She closed her eyes at the way his touch made her tighten lower and deeper inside. "No." She pressed against him for a moment, then backed away slightly.

"Where you going?"

Senada was operating on instinct. Her lungs weren't functioning all that well. She took a shallow breath. "I'm going to kiss your . . ." She put her mouth on his hard chest and felt him quiver beneath her.

He swore. "Don't stop," he said, pushing aside her bra and gently squeezing her breasts.

She hadn't been planning on it. Senada was on automatic sensual pilot. She wrapped her tongue around one flat male nipple and skimmed her hands over his stomach.

Troy made a strangled noise in the back of his throat.

"Like that?" she said, pulling his shirt out of his jeans.

He wrapped his hands around her rib cage and tugged her close, pulling her mouth upward. His eyes were nearly black with arousal, his nostrils flaring with the effort of his breath. Her bare breasts brushed against his chest. "I've never wanted to kiss a woman this much in my life."

Her heart jerked at his words and the sight of his bruised mouth. "You ca—"

He shifted her intimately against him and lowered his mouth to the tip of one of her breasts. The sight and feel of his mouth on her undid her. She closed her eyes. "You shouldn't. Your mouth. You'll hurt—"

He rocked against her intimately, and she went mindless.

"Ohhh." Her legs were wrapped around his hips, his erection pressing against where she was soft and wet. If they'd been without clothes, he would be inside her. The thought drove her mad, and she instinctively rubbed against his hard masculinity.

He moved and she moved in delicious, torturous, sensual friction that sent sparks through her nerve endings. His mouth barely glanced her breasts, but his tongue tasted and teased. Her hands flowed over his shoulders.

She felt him tug loose the button to her black jeans and push down the zipper, felt it but didn't quite comprehend it. When his fingers slid beneath her panties, to her moist femininity, however, she jolted in surprise.

"Calm down," he murmured. "Just want to touch you a little bit. Just a little bit."

His words cut through her protest, and he rubbed her until she was wet with wanting. Her mouth was dry, and she was always conscious of his hardened masculinity so close, yet so far. She was just about to tell him to stop when he thrust his finger inside her.

Senada gave an uncontrollable shiver.

"C'mon, Senada," he told her in a low, sexy voice. "Give it to me."

He thrust his finger inside her again, using his thumb against her swollen button of sensation. Another thrust and she spun out of control. Her inner muscles clenched in fits and starts, and she couldn't stop the sob of pleasure that broke from her throat.

She sank against his chest and gasped for breath. Good Lord! She couldn't remember when she'd had such a powerful release. Although stunned, she was aware of the evidence of his arousal pressed against her. Instinctively, she slid her hand down to cup him.

"Sin, no, you don't—"

She rubbed him through his jeans, skimming her fingernail down his zipper.

"Stop," he said, putting his hand over hers. "I don't want you doing this just because I—"

"Gave me a great climax." She unbuttoned his jeans, warming to the task. "One good time deserves another."

"No." He stayed her hand again, this time more firmly.

His violet eyes were serious. "I don't want you doing this out of some weird sense of gratitude. I did what I wanted to do, and you letting go was a gift."

Her heart swelled in her chest. Men always expected their turn, nearly always demanded it. Sometimes they wanted their turn first, every time. She almost didn't know how to take his response. He was still very hard. He obviously still wanted her. She tilted her head to one side and skimmed her hand down his chest to his abdomen, to the unfastened button.

"I never knew unselfishness could be so sexy, Troy." She looked up and held his gaze at the same time she deliberately lowered his zipper. She leaned forward and kissed his jaw. "There's my thank you." She slid her hand inside his briefs and watched his eyes darken. "This is because I want to."

Troy's only words after that were a mingling of curses and praise. Senada felt every one of his moans inside her. When he went over the edge, she held him tightly and wondered why she felt she'd never been more intimate with a man.

Late that night, Troy followed her up the walkway. He was a little off kilter. He couldn't remember a more powerful lovemaking experience, and they hadn't even been undressed. He was awash with emotion, amazement, arousal, affection, and a strange overwhelming protectiveness toward Sin.

She started to open the door, but he put his palm flat against it and lowered his swollen mouth to just behind her ear. "You okay?"

"Yeah." She turned around and looked at him, her dark eyes seeming even darker in the moonlight. "Are you?"

Her reciprocal question caught him off guard. He shook his head. "I don't know. Give me a few more minutes." He dipped his head, then looked back at her with a serious gaze. "Sin, I know something's going on with you. I know it's something—" he hesitated, then went on, "to do with your health. If you need—"

Senada's eyes widened in fear. "My health." She laughed, but the sound was forced. "Have you been hitting the tequila lately?" She turned back around. "I have a healthier lifestyle than I've ever had."

He put his hand on her shoulder. "C'mon Sin, you can tell me. Especially after tonight. After we—"

She shook her head and jammed the key into the lock. "My health is fine."

His heart tightened like a vise. "You don't have to do this alone. Let me in. Let me help. Let me closer."

"I let you get close earlier, Troy," she said, stepping through the doorway. "That should have been enough."

Frustration ate at him. "Well, it wasn't. I want to know the truth about what's going on. I want to know your secrets. I want to know everything."

She turned back to face him, her eyes sparking with emotion that rivaled his own. "You think you have the right to know my soul because of what happened tonight. Tonight was about two people who got real hot and took some pleasure. No strings, no rights, no promises. Don't be confused."

Her words hit him like a slap. He didn't know if he was more angry with the hurt he was feeling or her continued reluctance to come clean with him. "Excuse me," he said, hearing the sarcasm in his voice. "I forgot you don't know how to get emotionally involved with a man." Then he turned on his heel and headed back to his car.

Senada trembled and damned herself for her weakness. Letting the screen door swing shut, she watched him. Even in the dark, she could see the hurt and anger rising off him like steam.

"You don't know how to get emotionally involved with a man."

His words echoed off the corners of her mind. So true. It wasn't news-flash material, but his statement made her feel shallow. She'd never really felt that way before. She'd always steered clear of emotional involvement with men because she'd learned an important lesson when her father left her mother. Men don't stay.

Don't count on them, and your heart will be safe.

Troy wasn't like the other men she'd been involved with. Senada knew it in her head and gut. In her heart? She sighed, trembling again. She'd thought her heart was protected, immune. But she felt an odd ache in her chest that she'd never felt before.

Troy stayed away from the bar for the next two days. Too annoyed to be reasonable, he considered throwing the towel in and going back to Tennessee. Senada Calhoun was just plain hell on his nerves.

"I'm not getting anywhere," he told Brick on the phone as he paced from one end of his crummy little room to the other. "I hate this motel. I'm surprised the damn phone works. Nothing else does." Perspiration trickled down his back, and he swore under his breath.

"You haven't found out *anything*, anything at all?" Brick asked, the sound of a screaming baby in the background.

Troy pulled the phone away from his ear at the loud noise, then gingerly put it back. "For Pete's sake, give the kid a pacifier or something. She sounds as if you're pinching her."

"Lisa's worn out. Trying to take a nap. This one's teething. I'm pacing." He gave a heavy sigh. "Back to Senada. Lisa's getting antsy. I wouldn't put it past her to come down there herself. Have you got anything?"

Troy hesitated. "I might. Nothing definite. Don't tell Lisa, but I followed Senada to a doctor's clinic and a pharmacy where she picked up some prescriptions. Saw a wrapper for—" He stopped, suddenly reluctant to disclose the rest.

"A wrapper for what?" Brick prodded.

"Nothing," Troy said. "I haven't figured it out, yet. She seems healthy, conscious of her diet, and all that stuff. It's clear as mud right now."

"Listen Troy, if you really want to come back, you can. Sin's stubborn as hell, but I sure didn't think it would take this long to try to reason with her. I mean," he added dryly, "it's not as if *I* was the one trying to reason with her. She hates my guts."

"Not really," Troy corrected. "She just lets you think that because she likes to see you squirm. She knows Lisa is happy with you. Of course, she thinks all the Pendleton men are primitive, protective, and dense."

Brick snickered. "That's not totally bad. If she underestimates you, you can make it work in your favor."

"Yeah," Troy said, not convinced. "Listen, do you know anything about Sin's family background?"

"Not much," Brick said. "Lisa mentioned that Sin's mother died a long time ago, and Sin's never been close with her father, although I think Lisa said he's supposed to be loaded."

"Loaded?" Troy repeated.

"Yeah. Owns a bunch of land in Texas. A cattle ranch or something. I think."

Senada gazed into her closet, searching for the best dress to wear tonight. It was almost like selecting a weapon. Thumbing past the white shirtwaist dress and the bubblegum-pink flowing A-line, she hesitated at the black one. Although the barbecue would be held outside, guests would be dressed in everything from western attire to cocktail dresses.

The black dress.

Senada pulled it out and looked at it, a black form-fitting cotton knit that stretched to her calves. It might have been fairly conservative if not for the illusion sleeves and midriff, and the slit up the right leg.

Designed to drop a man at fifty paces, it was what she'd always referred to as her slut-for-a-night dress. Her father would hate it.

She chuckled under her breath. Well, that was good enough for her. She tossed it on the bed and reached for matching heels. It was too hot, so she would skip nylons.

Padding into the bathroom, she swung her hair up into a wide black onyx clip, then pulled out her eyeliner, mascara, and lipstick. If she really wanted to get her father's goat, she would haul out all the war paint, but even Senada was past that. Applying her makeup, she planned her jewelry. She would keep it simple and let her wicked dress do the talking.

She glanced at the little clock in the bathroom. Time for her blood test and insulin. She'd made progress. She could perform the blood test with a wince, and now she only squeaked when she gave herself the shot for the insulin. After that time Troy overheard her, she'd forced herself to get a grip.

Quick prick for the blood test. She pulled out the syringe and frowned. Sitting down on the closed commode, she measured two fingers over on her left thigh and fought the quick, sharp surge of horror. She took a deep breath, held it, then jabbed her thigh. "Oh!"

"Done, all done" she told herself, as if she were a nurse trying to soothe a child after a shot. She stood and caught sight of herself holding the needle in front of the mirror. The resemblance to her mother was strong, long dark hair, dark exotic eyes, and full lips. The stubborn chin and high cheekbones, however, came straight from her dad.

Senada looked at the syringe and considered the significance of it. One more reason, she thought, for her father to reject her. She was a fool to go tonight. But Senada was no stranger to doing something foolish, so she tossed the syringe and went to the bedroom to pull on her dress. She was just putting in her earrings as the doorbell rang. Troy. Her stomach fluttered and she scowled. She wasn't the stomach-fluttering type.

Stepping into her black high-heeled sandals, she walked to the door and opened it, not even glancing at Troy. "Come on in. I'll be just a minute," she said, turning back to her room. "Gotta grab my purse."

She threw a lipstick and a glucose stick in her purse. Great combination, she thought wryly, then reentered the living room. "Thanks for wait—" She broke off when she caught sight of Troy.

His broad shoulders were set off by a white, white shirt with a silver western slide. Black jeans molded his narrow hips and long legs to black boots. Topping it off was black hair, tanned skin, and searing violet eyes that were consuming her like a wildfire.

Senada felt scorched. She gave a little shake of her head. This was ridiculous. She swallowed and prayed for a little moisture in her mouth. "Hi," she said, nodding her head. "You look good. Didn't know Pendletons could do 'cowboy.' The only thing you're missing is the hat."

"We're adaptable." He flicked his gaze over her and stepped forward. "Who do you want to kill tonight?"

Senada shrugged, surprised again at his perceptiveness. "Why would you say that? I'm just out for a little fun," she said with a smile as she sauntered toward him. "Nothing wrong with having a little fun, is there?"

He stepped directly in front of her, put his finger under her chin, and stared straight into her eyes. "You're full of it, Sin. You're dressed like the feminine equivalent of a cocked gun, and you know it." He bent down to boldly brush a kiss over her lips. "But it'll be damn fun to watch. Let's go." He smiled, and his white teeth matched his shirt. "Angel."

Senada's laugh caught in her throat. She knew he was joking, but the last person who'd called her angel had been her mother. They got into the car, and he asked her a few questions about the Circle K Ranch. Senada gave short answers. The miles flew by, and the closer they drew to the ranch, the tighter the knot in her stomach grew. They turned into the entrance, and Senada took a quick breath.

Troy threw a questioning glance in her direction. "You okay?"

Senada sharply reined in her churning emotions. "Fine," she murmured, "just fine." She drank in the sight of the new fences, well-fed cattle, and new buildings. She gasped at the sight of the house. The addition was far larger than the original sprawling ranch.

Troy looked at her again. "Problem?"

She took a careful breath. She was going to

have to get a grip. "No problem," she said in a firm voice, hoping her insides would take the hint.

He parked in a graveled area, and Senada joined him as they walked toward the crowd gathered in the backyard.

"You know many of these people well?" Troy asked.

"Not really," she hedged. "Since I used to live in the area, I might end up seeing someone I knew from back then. But San Pedro's one of those towns that kids leave as soon as they graduate from high school."

He shrugged. "I guess Beulah County's the same way."

She smiled up at him. "But you stayed."

"And you came back to San Pedro."

"True." Senada sighed. "Not one of my most rational decisions," she murmured in a low voice. Her gaze swept past the tables of food and the band to the crowd of people. Her stomach knotted.

"Here comes your friend," Troy said, gesturing toward Chris Grant as he walked in their direction.

"Hello, beautiful," Chris said, taking Senada's hands in his. "How come you never dress like this at the bar?"

Senada laughed and shook her head. "Can't wear heels at work," she said, completely missing the point. "My feet would declare a mutiny."

Troy took a slow, careful breath. There was, after all, no rational reason for him to feel possessive. Holding on to a woman like Senada would be like trying to catch the wind.

Chris grinned and swept a half-glance over Troy. "You should have told me you needed a ride. I would have been glad to come and get you."

I'll just bet.

She backed up a step. "Troy didn't mind, did you?"

He slipped his arm around her waist. "Not at all. I love taking Senada for a ride."

Sin rolled her eyes. "You've got a lot of guests here tonight. Is the boss going to show?"

Chris's dispirited gaze clung to Troy's hand on Senada's hip. Troy decided it would take an act of God for him to remove it.

Chris adjusted his hat and shrugged. "I think Calhoun's supposed to make some kind of announcement."

Calhoun. Troy's attention snagged on Senada's last name.

"Is that so?" she asked. "Business or personal?"

"I dunno. He's being secretive. Listen, you help yourself to the food, and if you need anything, anything at all, you let me know."

"Thanks," Troy said, even though he knew Chris hadn't been talking to him. "We'll do that."

As soon as Chris left, he turned to Senada. "Who's this Calhoun guy?"

"His name's Rex. Rex Calhoun. I think I'd like to get some food," she said, and moved toward the tables.

"Any relation to you?" Troy continued, matching his stride to hers.

"Yes." Her face tightened and she walked faster, clearly unsettled by his questions.

Troy already knew the answers, but he wanted her to tell him. Silly, but there it was. "You gonna tell me what this is all about?"

Senada stopped midstride, staring toward the house where a middle-aged man and much younger blond woman walked down the steps together.

Troy narrowed his eyes and repeated the question. "You gonna tell me what this is all about?"

In that split second, her expression went from confident woman to vulnerable little girl and back again. "I think you'll find out soon enough."

SEVEN

Senada drank in the sight of her father. She was unprepared for the way her heart jerked. Rex looked older, but just as hard as ever. Still big and lean, he walked with the same arrogantly determined stride. Right now, however, he deferred to the woman by his side.

A flood of memories raced through her mind and deeper. As a little girl, she remembered running to hug him when he came home. He would scoop her up in his strong arms and tell her she had the softest cheek in Texas.

She absently touched her cheek with her hand.

He'd always liked teasing her, pretending he'd stolen her nose, making a scary face when she interrupted him while he read the paper. She'd thought he was the strongest, best man in the world. She'd worshipped him.

Until the year her mother died.

A chill passed over her.

"Sin," Troy said gently, "you want something to eat or drink?"

She blinked and looked at him. "I should get something. Let's go. The barbecue looks good, doesn't it?" Automatically filling her plate, she watched her father from the corner of her eye. His arm was around—She took a careful breath because she still couldn't believe it. His wife. He'd finally remarried. She'd always believed he wouldn't.

She took one bite of barbecue and drank water. Rex was making the rounds. She wondered what he would say when he saw her. He would recognize her, she thought, and she buried herself in the crowd like a coward. Suddenly she wasn't sure she was ready for this. Her head started to pound.

Troy came toward her wearing a concerned expression on his face. "I lost you. Sin, I know you think this is none of my business, but you don't look so good and—"

Someone let out a loud whistle. "Everybody listen up. Rex has got something to say."

Senada tensed. She felt a little shaky, and she hated herself for having such an emotional reaction.

"I'd like to make an announcement. The reason I'm having this little shindig is to celebrate the fact that there's going to be another Calhoun around here soon." He looked down at his wife. "Sheree's going to have a baby." He looked over the crowd with a broad cocky grin. "And we have reason to believe we'll be having a—" His gaze finally met Senada's, and he stumbled.

Senada took a gulp of water and wished with all her heart that it was Scotch.

"Having a what?" one of the hands prodded.

His wife laughed and shook her head. "First time I've seen Rex Calhoun speechless. Well, make that the second time. It looks like we'll be having a son."

Ah, a son, Senada thought bitterly. A son with none of her mother's errant genes. She lifted her cup as if to toast him, nodded, then turned away. "Time to go," she said to Troy. She dumped her plate in a trash can.

"Whoa," he said, reaching for her arm. "Things have just gotten started. Are you sure you want to go?"

"Absolutely positive." She shot a quick glance over her shoulder. Her father was being waylaid by many well-wishers, and that suited her just fine. She looked at Troy. "If you want to stay, I'll see if I can find a ride with someone else."

He looked exasperated. "I didn't say that. I just thought—"

She held up her hands. "I really don't have a problem with it." She would *walk* if she had to!

Troy took her other hand in his and brought

her up close. "Shut up for just a minute," he said in a low voice. "Don't you want to see your father?"

Tears sprang to her eyes. She squinted to keep them at bay. "I have seen him. I want to go. Now."

He took a deep breath. "You went to an awful lot of trouble to be here tonight."

"I'm ready to go." She worked hard to keep her voice level.

He nodded. "Okay."

Weak with relief, Senada could have kissed him for agreeing without any more questions. It took just a few minutes to walk to the car, but during that brief time, Senada felt more shaky, more nervous.

Troy opened the car door, and she just stared at it.

He looked at her. "Something wrong?"

She put her hand to her head. "I don't know." Her doctor had told her something about these symptoms. Her dietician had warned her.

"Senada!"

She heard her father call her name and wished she could teleport herself to anywhere else.

"Senada." He was out of breath when he reached her. His face was etched in shades of pain and hope. He shook his head. "Missy, it's been years."

She started to feel disoriented and swore. With her last remnant of sense, she reached in her purse and squirted the glucose in her mouth. "I need to sit down, Troy," she murmured, feeling his strong arms support her almost before she got the words out. "Insulin reaction."

The next few minutes were a blur. When her disorientation began to fade, her surroundings came into focus. Senada looked at the burgundy brocade sofa where she was reclining and wondered how she'd gotten there. She heard voices all around her, but couldn't quite make out what they were saying. "Could I have some water, please?"

She glanced up and her gaze meshed with Troy's. His violet eyes were concerned but steady. The steadiness calmed her.

He took her hand in his. "How you feelin'?"

"Better." She nodded. "Thirsty."

"We need some water in here," Troy said, over the other voices.

"Should we get her to the hospital?" she heard her father ask.

Senada shook her head and winced. Her dietician had warned her she could end up with a killer headache if she had an insulin reaction. "I'm okay. I just need to eat something soon. That's what got me into this mess to start with," she said darkly. She'd been too nervous to eat as much as she should have.

One of the domestic staff brought her water.

Senada thanked the woman and quickly drank it. She swung her feet off the sofa and sat up. Still shaky, but much better. "I think I'd like to go home now."

The voices went silent.

"Go home?" her father repeated, stepping in front of her. "What do you mean go home? For the first time in seven years, you *are* home."

His booming voice caused a familiar flutter of nerves inside her. It gave her a moment's pause before she caught herself. *She was an adult now.* "Actually, my *home* is in town. It's a nice little two-bedroom house on a quiet street. I like it very much."

Rex looked taken aback, then jutted out his stubborn jaw. "You're not going anywhere. You're sick."

A rage of anger, determination, and pride raced through her, stiffening her spine. She stood and met him eye to eye. "I'm not sick."

"You nearly fainted in my driveway." He gave a quick jerk of his head in Troy's direction. "Your boyfriend here had to carry you to the house. He damn well wouldn't let anyone else near you."

Her headache intensified. She didn't know which to argue first, Troy being her "boyfriend" or her fainting spell. She noticed her father looking at her dress and wondered if he was going to start in on that. "I think—"

"And what are you trying to do, wearing a dress like that? Start a riot?"

That tore it. "Well, of course. It's my goal in life to start a riot wherever I go."

Sheree, the young, pregnant wife, stepped closer to Rex and put her hand on his arm. "Now, Rex, it's been a long time since you and Senada have seen each other. You might want to try to keep your voice down and—"

"Keep my voice down!" he bellowed. "My daughter shows up for the first time in seven years in a see-through dress and nearly croaks on my driveway. And I'm supposed to keep my damn voice down!"

Senada shook her head and looked at Troy. "This is too much. Maybe," she said, and seriously doubted it at the moment, "maybe we can try to talk another time. Best wishes on your marriage and pregnancy, Sheree. Just in case you're concerned about the financial implications of my showing up, I haven't accepted any money from Rex since I graduated from college." She turned back to her father and gave a half smile. "Congratulations on your marriage and new baby, Daddy. I hope this time around you're happier."

She forced her feet into motion, headed for the front door. "I'd like to go now."

Troy was at her side, his arm at her waist before she could blink, and his strength made everything inside her sigh in relief. "Can we get out before my father starts again?" she whispered as she stepped through the doorway.

Troy nodded. "You want me to stop somewhere on the way home to get you something to eat?"

She got into the car and shook her head. "No. I'll just pull something out of the freezer. Won't take more than five minutes."

They drove in silence for several minutes, and Senada leaned her head back and closed her eyes. Troy finally broke the quiet. "It appears you and your father have had a volatile relationship."

She laughed lightly. "He's nitro. I'm glycerin. Doesn't take much to make us explode when we're together."

"So why did you pick tonight to go see him?"

"I thought it was time. Hoped things might be different. They weren't." She rolled her eyes. "Can't believe the timing for that insulin reaction. Couldn't have been worse."

Troy tugged his slide loose and pulled open his collar. "Gotta tell you, Sin, it scared me."

She frowned. "I'm sorry I got you involved in all this. You can drop me off and go try to forget about it."

"Yeah. Right," he said, as if he had no intention of doing any such thing.

"Really. Once I eat—"

"Forget it, Sin. I'm not going anywhere until

I'm sure you're okay. You can't tell me you weren't a little scared, yourself."

"A little," she admitted. "But panic is one of the symptoms. I was prepared because both the doctor and my dietician had drilled me on what to do in case of an insulin reaction. It wouldn't have happened if I'd eaten, but I was too upset about seeing my father to eat."

Troy pulled the car to a stop in front of her house. "Then let's take care of that first."

He walked her to the front door, then urged her into a chair next to the table.

"This isn't necessary," Sin began, standing. "I can do—"

"Sit down." He pulled two microwave meals out of the freezer. "Pick one."

Senada pointed her finger at one and glared at him. "You know, I really don't like bossy men. I never have. It's part of the reason I don't get along with my father."

Troy tossed the meal in the microwave and punched in the time. He turned back to her with a determined smile. "Just think of me as the exception to the rule." Within a few short minutes, the timer dinged, and Troy brought her the meal with a sugar-free drink. Her emotional state made her want to toss it, but she forced herself to take small bites.

"You want to talk about any of this?" Troy asked.

"Not really." She put another bite in her mouth.

"How long have you known you had diabetes?"

Reluctant to answer because she knew it would reveal too much, she hesitated, then shrugged. "Since right before I left Chattanooga."

She braced herself for a barrage of questions and accusations, but Troy just studied her silently and nodded. He extended his hand to her forehead as if he intended to stroke back her hair, but apparently thought better of it. "Finish your meal. I'll go run your bath water."

She stared after him. "How did you know I wanted a bath?"

"My sister Carly taught me a few things, and one of them is a woman's belief in the power of a bath," he said over his shoulder as he kept walking toward the bathroom. Senada finished the rest of her food and tried to block out all her feelings about her father. The pain and joy she'd experienced upon seeing him. The secret hope that finally everything could be right between them. The terrible disappointment that came from seeing that they still operated under the same old communication guidelines. Wild assumptions and no trust.

Just the *sound* of the running water was soothing to her, an invitation to wash away all her hurt and confusion. She kicked off her shoes and walked to the bathroom.

Troy leaned against the doorway and gave a half grin. "Need some help?" he asked lightly.

Despite the fact that she was tired and emotionally used up, the offer made her stomach dip. No clever comments came to mind, so Senada did something unusual. She was completely honest. She stepped closer to him and looked into his face. "You're a very kind man, Troy. I don't understand why you put up with me." She pressed her mouth to his and gently rubbed back and forth, wanting to absorb something from him, wanting to give at the same time.

Her breath grew short, and she pulled back. "I don't know why you put up with me," she whispered. "But I'm really glad you did tonight." She licked her lips, and the taste of him teased her senses. "Thanks."

When she closed the door behind her, Troy licked his own lips and groaned. Loosening a few more buttons on his shirt, he walked to the living room and tried not to picture Sin, wet and nude, in that bathtub. He flicked on the TV and channel surfed until he found a ballgame. After forty minutes passed with no sign of Sin, however, he started to wonder.

He went to the hallway and stared at the closed door for a long moment. "Hey, Sin, you okay in there?"

He heard a little splash. "Yeah," she called back. "I must have fallen asleep."

"Good idea," he said with a chuckle. "Except your bed might be a better place for it."

She made an unintelligible grumbly noise.

"You need a robe or anything?"

"No. It's on the door."

He heard some more splashing followed by curses. Biting his tongue to keep from checking on her again, he leaned against the wall and waited. More splashing and more curses. She let out a groan of frustration.

"Troy," she finally called.

"Yes." He moved to stand directly outside the door.

"I'm having a little problem."

"Yes?"

"Standing." She hesitated. "My legs have turned to spaghetti."

He squeezed the bridge of his nose. His brothers would find this situation enormously funny. He wished he did. "You want me to help you get out?"

She waited a long moment. "Yes, please," she said in a low voice.

"Okay," he muttered, and braced himself. Somebody somewhere was going to pay big for this. He pushed open the door, expecting to find her trying to cover herself with her arms or a washcloth or the shower curtain.

No such luck. Her skin was rich, creamy, and tan, and he could see *all* of it. From her flushed cheeks, past her vulnerable throat and delicate shoulders, to her full breasts, inviting hips, and shapely thighs all the way to her painted toenails, the sight of her, naked and accessible, could have brought him to his knees. Her eyes were smoky and heavy-lidded as if she were aroused, but Troy knew she was just completely and totally exhausted.

Of its own volition, his gaze dipped to her wet breasts and dusky rose erect nipples. A dozen unfulfilled fantasies scorched his mind. He mentally swore and ignored the beads of perspiration forming on his forehead.

He cleared his throat. "I'll get you a towel." He snatched the pink terry bath sheet from the rack and draped it over his shoulder. He thought about throwing it over her now, but he'd just end up drenching it. "I'll, uh, put my hands under your arms."

She lifted her hands.

Troy's heart stopped. Such a simple gesture, but it exhibited something Sin rarely, if ever, gave. Trust.

He sucked in a deep breath, put his hands under her arms, and started to lift her. She was deadweight. "It's okay if you want to push up with your legs a little."

"I'm trying." She made a sound of frustration and splashed. She slipped, he held tight, she reached desperately for his shoulders. Then she was out of the tub, and her naked slippery body was pressed tortuously against his.

Troy stopped. He couldn't ignore the sensation of her nipples scoring his chest. His shirt and pants were instantly moistened by her. Troy couldn't help thinking how hot and wet she'd be, and how easy it would be to touch her, how easy it would be to slip inside her and lose himself.

He ground his teeth together.

"Sorry," she murmured. "Guess I'm a little slippery."

"I'll say," he muttered. "Let's get this towel around you." He tried to shift so that he could wrap it around her, as much for his sanity as for her comfort. He shifted again, and she wiggled against him, her breasts abrading his wet shirt, her lower body against his crotch.

Troy swore. "Forget it," he said, and swung her into his arms. The position put her breasts about six inches from his mouth, but he wasn't going to think about that, he told himself. Not in the seconds it would take to carry Sin to her bedroom.

"Sorry," she said again as he stomped toward her bed.

"It's okay," he lied. "I'm glad I can help." Certain his hands were going to permanently attach themselves to her skin, he tumbled her on the bed more quickly than he'd planned and put the towel over her.

He turned away and willed his body not to shudder in arousal. "Which drawer?" he asked in a voice curt to his own ears.

"Drawer?" she echoed.

"Which drawer is your nightgown in?"

A long silence followed. "I, uh, don't really have to have a nightgown. I don't always wear—"

Troy shook his head. "Wear one tonight." When she didn't answer, he looked over his shoulder. "I'm staying."

She looked dismayed. "That's not necessary. I'll be—"

"I'm staying. Which drawer?"

Senada sighed. "Lord, you're bossy. Third one on the left."

Troy immediately pulled out the drawer and sank his hands into a plethora of silk and satin. Why didn't somebody just shoot him? *What did you expect, bonehead?* he asked himself. *Cotton and flannel?*

He grabbed a pink silky something with straps and slung it in her direction. "Here. Want something to drink?"

"Some water would be nice."

Troy walked to the kitchen, poured Sin a glass of water, and just stood there and watched the water pour from the faucet.

He was hot, bothered, and hard with no sign of release or relief in the long night ahead.

Cool water. Cool, mind-clearing, soothing water.

Troy stuck his head under the faucet.

EIGHT

Troy walked back into her room. "Sin," he began, then stopped when he saw that she was asleep.

A dry chuckle rumbled from his throat. The woman clearly didn't like to be told what to do. She was beneath the covers, her face as innocent as an angel's, as trusting as a child's. Her body, however, would tempt Saint Peter. And Troy was certain her body was presently nude, because the rose-colored scrap of silk lay on top of the covers.

He sighed and took a sip of the water, then placed it on the bedside stand. He looked at Sin and felt a tugging sensation. Asleep, with her guard down, and her sharp weaponry of wit put away, she was more accessible. Her defenses weren't fifteen feet high. He wondered how long the walls stayed down when she woke up. He wondered what it would be like to be with Sin when all her walls were down. He wondered what it would take for her to let a man near her without her defenses firmly in place.

He wondered how he was going to walk away now that he knew some of her secrets.

Shaking his head, he scooped up her rose-colored lingerie and carried it with him as he strolled toward her bedroom window. She was technically fine, he told himself. Most men would consider their duty done. He should be able to go.

No way in hell, he thought. Especially after he'd watched her deal with both her father and the insulin reaction. Her skin had turned so pale, and she'd been so close to passing out, she'd nearly scared the spit out of him.

Rustling the silky nightgown between his fingers, he decided he would leave as soon as she woke in the morning. Her perfume taunted his nostrils, and he looked at the feminine garment in his hand. He wondered when she'd last worn it. He wondered who had taken it off.

Swearing, he looked at the moon for answers and knew he'd find none. But it was deep in the night, and Troy would stay and do what he should. He'd done it before, just never with a woman who turned him on his ear. He'd done it for his sister, Carly, for his brothers and his new sisters-in-law, even once for his nephew, Luke,

ESCAPE...
Into Romance and
Embrace Special Savings.

Get **4** New

Romance Novels
FREE!

See inside for details...

Hurry!
Offer
Available
For A Limited
Time Only

Lose Yourself In 4 Steamy Romances and Embrace A World Of Passion — Risk Free!

Here's An Offer To Get Passionate About:

Treat yourself to 4 new, exclusive romances free. If you enjoy the heart-pounding and sultry tales of true love, keep them with our compliments.

Along with your 4 FREE books you'll receive 4 more Loveswept books to preview risk-free for 15 days. You may keep this trial shipment and pay only $2.66 each*.

Then, should you fall in love with Loveswept and want more passion and romance, you can look forward to 4 more Loveswept novels arriving in your mail, about once a month. These dreamy, passionate romance novels are hot off the presses, and from time to time will even include special edition Loveswept titles at no extra charge.

Your No-Risk Guarantee

Your free preview of 8 Loveswept novels does not obligate you in any way. If you decide you don't want the books, simply return any 4 of them and owe nothing. There's no obligation to purchase, you may cancel at any time.

All future shipments come with a 15-day risk-free preview guarantee. If you decide to keep the books, pay only our low regular price of $2.66 per book*. That's a savings of 24% off the current cover price of $3.50. Again, you are never obligated to buy any books. You may cancel at any time by writing "cancel" across our invoice and returning the shipment at our expense.

*Plus shipping & handling, sales tax in New York, and GST in Canada.

Get 4
Loveswept Romances
FREE!

Get 4 Loveswept Romances

FREE!

No Risk. No obligation to purchase. No commitment.

when the little boy was sick with an earache and Troy's brother was out of town.

He leaned against the window, knowing he would change positions many times before dawn. Troy settled in for a night watch. This time, he watched Sin as she slept.

Senada saw her mother in the casket, so beautiful but forever still, and she felt the unbearable pain again. "Mama, please don't go! Please." She shook her head at the woman, who tried to calm her. "No. She mustn't go. I can't let her leave!"

Grief and fear twisted inside her. Tears burned her eyes. She blinked, and it was no longer her mother in the beautiful casket. It was Senada. "No!" she screamed.

"You're dreaming," she distantly heard the male voice. "Wake up," he said again, and she felt a firm shake.

Sin opened her tear-moistened eyes and stared straight into Troy's concerned gaze. Realization flooded her. Relief followed. Sweet relief and a comfort that had been sorely missing from her life. She felt something strange and new, couldn't label it for the long moment that his gaze held hers.

Trust, a faint voice echoed through her. Senada went still. Trust? She *trusted* Troy Pendleton.

She was insane.

Uncertainty made her heart skip. Not Troy, she told herself. "Ohhhh." She covered her face with her hand. "Sorry I screamed," she muttered for what felt like the tenth time.

"No need," he said, and offered her a glass of water. Senada drained the glass.

"Bad dream about your mother?"

She nodded, pulling the sheet up around her shoulders. "She died when I was twelve." She hesitated for a moment, then finished with a shrug. "Complications of diabetes."

He nodded slowly in comprehension. "Tough age to lose a parent."

"You would know," she said, recalling how the Pendletons had lost both their parents within a few years of each other.

"My mom died when I was eight. I was a little older than twelve when my father passed away."

"My father abandoned my mother the year before she died. He couldn't handle her illness," she blurted out, though she wasn't sure why.

"And that's why you two don't get along real well," he said, adjusting her pillow. "You hate his guts for that, don't you?"

She opened her mouth to protest but couldn't. "In a way, I guess I have. I've never forgiven him for not being there when she needed him."

"His not being there put a lot more of the burden on you, didn't it?"

She shook her head. "That wasn't the point. She needed him."

"There's more to it than that," he said. "I don't know all the psycho-babble, but Carly's always talking about how we need to be aware that our communication patterns are affected by our upbringing, and that children who lose their parents are angry about a lot of things. They're angry because they've been abandoned, and they're angry because they feel like their childhood has been stolen."

Senada just stared at him. Troy Pendleton, Mr. Insensitivity, had just nailed feelings she'd always kept secret. She was caught between resentment and admiration for his perceptiveness.

He tucked a finger under her chin. "Tell the truth. What did you do that last year your mother was alive?"

Sin looked away from him. Even in the darkness, they were too intense, too probing. "I went to school every day," she said, remembering those days when the sun had never seemed to shine, when she'd never felt like smiling. "I played with a friend every once in a while," she continued, trying to add a note of normalcy when there'd been none.

"How often?" he asked.

She shot him an impatient glance and sat up, grasping the sheet just before it fell below her breasts. "Okay. Not very often. I fixed dinner, did the laundry, and sat on the bed with her every night. She was too weak to do anything else."

"This is probably gonna tick you off, but did you ever go for counseling?"

"Not until it was too la—" Senada broke off. "Years later when I got in a little trouble in high school, my father made me go see a psychologist. I didn't want to be there," she said, looking back at him. "So it wasn't a successful experience."

"Trouble in high school?" he asked, lifting a dark brow.

Senada smiled. "You don't sound surprised. What kind of trouble are you expecting me to say?" She leaned forward. "Mooning the principal? I never got caught at that. Making out under the bleachers while I skipped Spanish? Never got caught at that either."

She watched the reluctant flame flicker to life in his eyes and felt a decadent thrill. The sensation was a nice diversion, but she should throw him out of her house, certainly off her bed. Her gaze dropped to his open shirt, revealing his bare muscular chest, and she withheld a sigh.

"You know, Sin, you make a man wonder just what it takes to *catch* you."

The thrill bucked through her again, stronger this time. "But that's part of the fun,

Troy, tagging, holding, but never quite catching."

Tempted and wanting to tempt, she leaned closer until her lips were a breath away from his. "Wanna have a little fun?"

He took the dare and her mouth in a searing kiss. "No," he said. "I wanna have a lot of fun. But you're in no shape for—"

Senada let the sheet drop from her breasts.

Troy's gaze fell to her bare torso.

Sin smiled. "You were complaining about my shape."

Troy dragged his gaze back to her eyes and shot her a dark look. "I wasn't complaining."

"That's nice."

He studied her thoughtfully. "What do you want, Sin? A diversion? A little vacation from your pain? Escape from reality?"

She sucked in a quick breath. Her bravado disappeared. His words made her feel unbearably exposed, worse than naked. She drew back. "Forget it. Just forget it. I shouldn't have—"

He wrapped his hand around her wrist. "Just answer the question, Sin. What do you want?"

Her heart hurt as it pounded in her chest. "I want to forget," she whispered. "Just for a little while. I want to forget."

He shook his head slightly, his violet eyes full of compassion and something deeper, something she'd never seen in a man's eyes before.

"Oh, sweetheart," he murmured, pulling her into his arms.

Senada fought tears. No one had ever called her sweetheart. Her breasts brushed his chest at the same moment his mouth took hers, and lightning mixed with tenderness. The combination was irresistible.

She stretched her hands around his shoulders and sighed into his mouth. Trust flowed through her again. Troy would make her forget, if only for a little while.

He pulled away from her for a moment to gaze at her. He took a deep breath. His eyes looked nearly black. "Are you sure?" he asked in a low, rough voice.

His concern grabbed at her so hard, she had to close her eyes. "Yes," she managed. "But you've got to stop being so kind or I'm going to cry."

He gave a half chuckle and rubbed her breasts from side to side against his chest. "You've been hangin' around the wrong kind of men."

Her nipples budded against the abrasion. "You might be able to convince me of that."

He tilted her chin upward and slid his tongue down her neck.

Her body suffused with heat. "Oh!"

His mouth continued its sensual trek down to the upper rise of one of her breasts. "Yes?" he murmured.

He licked gently, precisely over the place where her heart beat furiously. Yet another tender but unbearably arousing gesture. "Yesss," she managed, and put her fingers through his hair to urge his mouth lower.

When his lips fastened on her nipple, she arched her back. His hands were on her arms, but she would almost swear that with each sweep of his tongue, he was stroking her secret places. Under his persistent caresses, she grew hot and uncomfortable. It was difficult to remain still.

She tugged at his shirt. "You have on too many clothes."

"Average amount," he corrected, moving his mouth to her other breast.

"Too many," she repeated, and started on his belt.

Her fingers brushed against his obvious arousal, and she had a tough time deciding whether to touch him now or to wait. Just for fun, she ran her fingernail down his zipper.

He sucked in a shallow breath. "If you don't move your hands away, you're gonna get something started."

She laughed through the achy fire in her blood. "I'm doing my best."

Troy swore and wrapped her hands around his waist. "What am I gonna do with you?"

"Keep me busy," she said. "Keep me very busy." She ran her tongue around his lips, then boldly slipped it inside his mouth.

It seemed a second later that he was cradling her head in one arm, supporting her back with the other as he pressed her down and kissed her long and luxuriously. As if he were determined to keep a check on the speed and velocity of their desire, he held her firmly.

Senada wanted the speed. She strained against him, slipping her hand between their bodies to cup him. "You have on too many clothes."

He shook his head, rubbing his lips back and forth across hers. "Don't wanna rush."

"Rush."

He chuckled low and sexy and nuzzled her neck. "You need to learn to take things slow and easy."

"I want you now." She did. Her body was hot, her breasts were swollen, and lower, she was wet and empty. She stroked him through his jeans.

He moaned and shifted away. "We can't do this fast tonight, Sin. There's too much of you I need to touch." He slid his hand down to her hip and squeezed. "Too much I want to kiss." He dipped his head and suckled the tip of one of her breasts.

Heady need raced through her. "Troy," she whispered.

"I'll take care of you. Trust me."

He began to play her body like a piano. His hands alternately taunted and teased, sending ripples of desire through her. She felt his mouth and breath whisper across her skin, then he left her feeling scorched with the trace of his tongue.

He kept his jeans on way too long, but she found herself struggling for a way to express her feelings. She kissed his chest, licked his nipples, put a love bite on his abdomen that made him swear.

"When are you taking off your jeans?" she demanded, feeling her control begin to slip.

"In a minute," he promised.

"You said that be—"

His fingers found her core, and she gasped. Slipping one finger inside her, he toyed with her center of pleasure with his thumb at the same time he slid his tongue inside her mouth. She moved against him, her body tightening beneath his persuasion. She resisted the crest, fought it. She wanted him with her, wanted him as out of control as she felt.

But then he moved down her body, spreading her thighs with his hands, and he took her with his mouth. With an avid intimate kiss, he consumed her resistance. His tongue was soft and wicked, his lips hungry, as if he couldn't get enough of her.

The thought and sensation were too much. Beyond her control, her climax yanked her up and over. She shuddered beneath him again and again until she was weak. Troy continued until

she pushed at him breathlessly. "Stop," she
whispered. "Stop."

He lifted his head, his eyes heavy-lidded, and
licked his lips. It was such an unaffected sensual
gesture that Senada closed her eyes. A second
passed, and she felt his breath on her face. Finding purpose despite the chaos inside her, she
looked at him. The tenderness and passion in his
eyes rocked her as much as her climax had.
Senada had never wanted to please a man more.

"Sin," he began. "I—"

She placed her trembling fingers over his
lips. "Your turn, wouldn't you say?"

She tilted her head so that her mouth
meshed with his. He tasted of passion and her,
and despite his strength, she tasted his need. He
wanted more than release, more than sex, more
than passion. At another moment the power of
his want would have daunted her. She would
have had to turn away.

Now she couldn't, and Senada suspected this
would take more than she'd ever given before.

"You're an incredible man," she told him,
then gave a soft chuckle. "But since you're a
Pendleton, you probably already knew that."

She nibbled at his neck, allowing her breasts
to sweep against his chest. She rubbed the inner
seam of his jeans with her index finger all the
way to his crotch. When he shifted his pelvis
against her, she smiled.

"Like that?"

"Yeah."

She unfastened the button and zipper and slipped her hand around him. He was hard; she felt the first drops of his arousal and rubbed them around the tip of his erection.

He sucked in a short breath.

"Like that?" she whispered, turned on by turning him on. She lifted her moistened finger to her lips.

Troy swallowed audibly. "Yeah." His voice was rough.

She leaned closer and skimmed her tongue all the way down his abdomen to his hardness. She kissed him intimately, then took him into her mouth.

Troy swore.

She tasted him, made love to him as he sifted his hands through her hair and continued to croon and swear. It was the sweetest, most erotic sound.

"Sin," he said, his voice unsteady. "I don't wanna go this way. Wanna be . . ."

She looked up at him. "Wanna be where?"

"Inside you."

Her heart jerked. For Troy, it clearly wasn't a matter of dominating her or owning her. It was a matter of needing to join himself with her. She felt a quickening inside herself. "Let's get rid of those jeans. All the way this time."

They both worked at the bottom half of his

clothes. He pulled a celophane packet from his pocket.

"How long have you had that?" she asked, idly curious.

His violet eyes held hers. "Since the first time we kissed. Problem?"

She felt a tumbling sensation. "No."

And the waiting was over. His mouth fastened on hers, and they tussled on the bed. First he was on top, then she. They stroked and urged and licked and moaned.

Then finally they found common ground on their sides. He lifted her thigh outside his hip and in one sure movement, he thrust inside her.

His groan echoed inside her.

"Oh, yes," she whispered.

He gave a sexy tilt of his pelvis and sank deeper. "Like that?" he said in a none-too-steady voice.

"Oh, yes," she managed back, stroking him with her inner muscles. "And you?"

"Oh, yes." He pulled back slightly, perspiration forming on his brow. Then he thrust again.

Senada closed her eyes. He made her feel so full. So full, she might even believe all her empty places would never be empty again.

"Open your eyes, sweetheart. I need to see you."

Senada immediately looked at him. His words stroked her heart. His body stroked her body. The combination was irresistible.

Slowly, as he pumped inside her, he lowered his mouth to hers and rolled her to her back. She smiled beneath his kiss. "Gotta be on top," she said, her laughter sneaking through her voice. "Gotta dominate. Gotta—"

"No," he said against her lips, and slipped his hand between them. "I just thought you might like a little support when you fly through the air."

Sin laughed again. Men loved to brag. She opened her mouth to retort, but his fingers unerringly found her most sensitive spot. The sensation was mind-boggling. "Ohhh."

There was no easy buildup this time, a quick spike of pleasure, and she was bucking beneath him, reaching for her pleasure, striving for his. She moved in fluid counterpart to his thrusts and watched his face tighten even as she tightened around him.

He swore, and she pulled his hips toward her.

"Sin," he murmured. "Sweetheart."

She arched against him at the same second she felt him come apart inside her. The physical pleasure was incredible, but his endearment reverberated in her heart long after they caught their breath and fell asleep in each other's arms.

Troy woke the next morning feeling as if he'd been through a battle. His muscles were sore, his mouth was dry, and there were little marks of Sin's lovemaking on his chest and stomach. He didn't have to look next to him to know she wasn't still in bed. He felt it. Her warmth was gone.

The thought disturbed him, and he raised up to sit on the side of the bed. He did a double take at his stomach and shook his head at the hickey on his abdomen. Knowing Sin, she'd probably left one on his thigh.

Hearing a soft groan in the bathroom, he pulled on his jeans and walked toward the source of the sound. The door was cracked, so he nudged it open.

Her hair a riot of sex-mussed waves, she wore her silky robe. Her kiss-swollen lips were set in a scowl, and in her hand, she held a syringe.

Her gaze met his, and Troy immediately saw that all the wonder from the night had been washed away from her eyes. She looked unhappily determined. Her defenses were firmly back in place.

She gave a sad tight smile. "You know what they say. There's got to be a morning after."

NINE

Troy crossed his arms over his chest and leaned against the doorjamb. "Mind if I watch?"

She stared at him. "Watch what?"

"Watch you give yourself your injection."

She started to shake her head before he even finished. "Yes, I do mind." She stepped closer to him and waved her hands as if to shoo him away.

He didn't budge. "Why? It'll be educational."

"Get someone else to educate you. This is *not* one of my favorite things to do. Go," she said, and waved her hand again. "Go, go, go."

"What's the big deal? You've been doing it for over two months now?"

"Get out of my bathroom, Troy. This is not a dignified performance."

He sighed and stepped backward. She quickly closed the door in his face.

Troy rubbed his hand through his hair and trudged back to the bedroom. He would never understand her. Never in a million years. He'd just been trying to help her to be a little more open about the diabetes and her treatment. After the previous night, he would have thought—

"Oh!"

He stopped abruptly at her yelp. "Sin?" When she didn't respond, he cocked his head toward the bathroom. "Sin, you okay?"

"Fine," she said in a desperately cheerful voice. "Fine and dandy." She whipped out of the door, her eyes glittering. "It's one of those experiences that is always new. Always fresh. Always like the very first time." She took a quick breath. "If you want to take a quick shower, go ahead. I'll see what I can get us for breakfast."

Then she flitted past him to the kitchen. Troy shook his head. Good thing he wasn't the sensitive type, or he would be downright offended by her behavior. She was acting as if they hadn't spent the night together, hadn't made love, hadn't touched. It was a damn good thing he wasn't stupid enough to fall in love with the woman. A damn good thing, he thought, and felt a sharp discomfort in the left side of his chest, right behind his rib cage.

When she saw Troy lift his eyebrow in inquiry about the difference in his food and hers,

Senada nodded. "I really have to limit the fat in my diet, not because of weight. I usually stick to cereal and fruit in the morning, sometimes a bagel."

Troy dug into his scrambled eggs. "Do you have someone who helps you plan your meals?"

"A dietician." She took a bite of her cereal.

"How often do you see your doctor?"

"Once a month."

"What all do they want you to do?"

She'd been wondering when he would grill her, she thought as she ate her cereal. She would answer his questions, and then tell him to mind his business. "Test my blood at least twice a day and keep a record of the results. Take the insulin twice a day. Stick to the diet. Eat every four hours. Avoid getting injured. Exercise," she added with a grimace. "And limit my chocolate intake."

Troy paused. "That one was the worst, wasn't it?"

She gave a half chuckle. "What makes you say that?"

He looked confused. "But that chocolate cupcake? Why were you eating it?"

"I negotiated for that chocolate cupcake. First chocolate I'd eaten in a month."

Realization crossed his face. "And I ate it." He grinned slowly. "It's a wonder you didn't kill me."

"I considered it."

He looked at her thoughtfully. "Why did you leave Chattanooga?"

Senada drank a sip of her milk. It was much easier discussing the physical aspects of her disease than the emotional, especially since she didn't have all the answers yet herself. "I'm not totally sure. Finding out I had it freaked me out. They put me in the hospital for a few days to regulate my medication and educate me. I told Lisa I was going away. While I was in the hospital, I just didn't see how I could go back to the status quo. Everything seemed as if it had been turned upside down. I thought of my mother and father. The only family I had left was my father, so I guess I was running to him. But once I got here, I came to my senses. My father is not the kind of man to run to in a crisis."

"Because of how he handled your mother's death," Troy said.

"Because of how he *didn't* handle it," she corrected.

"Have you thought about going back to Tennessee?"

"No." She didn't pause. She glanced down at her empty bowl and wondered when she'd finished. "I have a lot of privacy here. If Lisa had known about the diabetes, she would have worried me to death. I couldn't handle that. I've been on my own too long to have someone, even someone as sweet as Lisa, looking over my shoulder."

"You really hate to depend on other people, don't you?"

He made it sound as if something was wrong with her because of her independence. She lifted her chin. "I prefer to make my own way," she told him. "In everything."

He surprised her by slipping his fingers through hers. "But some things take two, Sin."

She'd wondered when he would remind her of their breathtaking intimacy. She'd done her best not to think about it. Her feelings were too strong. "True, but I can do most things for myself. By myself."

He tilted her chin up, compelling her to meet his gaze. "Why do I get the impression you're running from me?"

Her heart tripped over itself. "I don't know," she hedged. "Why?"

"Because you've barely looked at me, and you haven't touched me after we made the stars come out last night."

"We had sex," she said in a low voice.

"We made love," he corrected.

"Troy," Her chest felt achy. She looked away, tried to remove her hand from his, but he wouldn't allow it. She cleared her throat. "We made love, and I want to thank you for being there for me last night. Last night was—" she sighed, "difficult for me. But what we did last night doesn't mean you need to act differently toward me. I don't expect things between us to change. You don't need to feel like you've got to look after me."

"So you expect me to go on as if we weren't together last night," he said.

"Yes."

"You're funny, Sin." He gave a rough chuckle. "Real funny."

"Troy," she began.

He shook his head. "Sweetheart, I told you before, you've been hanging around the wrong kind of man."

"And I suppose you're the *right* kind," she said, her tone skeptical.

"Yeah, but when all you've done is hang around the bad guys, sometimes you have a hard time identifying the good guys."

Soon after that, she kicked him out. She did it nicely, but she still showed him the door.

"I'll see you tonight," he told her. "You're working, aren't you?"

"Yes." She paused. "Thank you."

"For?" he prodded.

"For everything."

The hint of huskiness in her voice was a balm to the raw feeling inside him. "You had a . . . demanding evening last night. Wouldn't hurt you to take it easy today."

Her lips twitched. "You're not trying to look after me, are you?"

"Not me," Troy said, then took advantage of her brief silence to kiss her.

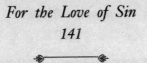

Senada finished talking with the waitress, and Troy came up beside her.

"How are you tonight?" he asked.

"Great. How about you?" She waved to a customer.

"Good." He shifted slightly on his feet. "How long has it been since you've eaten?"

She glanced at her watch. "About three hours. You?"

Troy blinked. "I don't know. I had some peanuts a few minutes ago."

She smothered a smile and nodded.

"You still look a little tired around your eyes. Are you sure you got enough rest today?"

Sin stifled a groan and leaned closer to him. She should have known Troy Pendleton's protectiveness instinct would go ballistic once he learned her secret. "You're hovering," she said, and walked toward the kitchen.

Troy followed her. "I'm not hovering."

"Oh?"

"Just asking a few questions."

"Uh-huh." She stopped at her office door. "Well, I answered them. Are you happy now?"

Troy sighed. "You know Sin, you have a big problem with people being concerned about you."

His statement jabbed at her. Her dietician had once said something similar. "Ever thought it might be your problem? That you might be a little too protective?"

"No."

Damn his self-assurance, she thought. "Well, if you'll excuse me, Troy, it's time for my insulin. Despite the fact that you don't think I can take care of myself, I'm managing quite nicely. And before you ask, I'll be eating a sandwich and some fresh vegetables in about thirty minutes. Would you also like to know how many squares of toilet paper I use when I go to the bathroom?"

He looked down his nose at her. "You gotta smart mouth, Sin."

She stretched her mouth in a suggestive smile. "After last night, you certainly oughta know."

A couple of hours later, Senada closed up the bar. Troy followed her home, left his nagging protectiveness at the door, and he made the stars fall again.

Senada technically didn't invite Troy to stay with her every night after that, but he did sleep with her, and he did stay with her. Every morning when she went to take her insulin, he asked if he could watch. And every time, she said no.

"I'm gonna go get some groceries for Maria and the kids," Troy told her a few days later.

Senada shook back her damp hair and looked at him. "Let me go with you."

He shrugged, fighting the secret delight he felt just being with her. "Okay."

They went to the grocery store and argued.

"Marshmallow Crunchies," Troy said. "You can't expect kids to eat that other stuff. Tastes like bark."

"You're not the one who'll have to deal with the sugar fit they'll have once they eat it."

"Okay. Compromise." Troy took the box of cereal from her hand and tossed it into the cart. "One box of bark. One box of Marshmallow Crunchies," he said with a grin, and tossed his box into the cart too. "Wonder which box will still be here at Christmas."

They rounded the corner and Troy brightened. "Cookies!"

Senada groaned.

They negotiated down from four varieties to two, then tackled meat, produce, and dairy products. Troy counted it a major victory that he managed to get the Fudgsicles past her. He accomplished that by finding some sugar-free Fudgsicles made by the same company and buying them for Senada.

"We bought way too much," she said as they stopped in front of Maria's house.

"Negotiations can be expensive." He got out of his car and grabbed four of the six bags. "If you hadn't been such a nag about nutritious stuff—"

"You would have ended up with three bags of Twinkies," she retorted, picking up the other two bags and following him to the door.

"Nag, nag, nag," he said, and bussed her with a quick kiss. He grinned at her stunned expression. "I never knew grocery shopping could be such fun."

Her eyes softened slightly. "Me neither."

She could have knocked him over with her little finger. He almost asked her to repeat herself, but Maria came to the door.

"Troy!" Maria's face lit with pleasure. "What have you done?"

"Senada and I picked up a few things for you at the grocery store. Can we come in?"

Sin saw just a tinge of disappointment come and go in Maria's eyes when the young mother turned to her. "Senada, how kind. *Gracias.* Please do come in. The children will be delighted to see you."

The children barely gave Troy time to put down the groceries before they climbed on him.

Senada helped Maria put the groceries away.

"The kids love him," Maria said, nodding in Troy's direction. "They haven't really had a man around in years. Especially such a good man."

Senada watched Troy get down on the floor with Rocky and Angel. "Sometimes, I think he's a boy, just bigger."

Maria shook her head. "Oh, no. Troy's all man."

Senada did a double take. Did Maria have a little crush on Troy, or was it a case of hero worship because he'd given her family a place to live? "Did you know he has six brothers?"

Maria's eyes rounded. "Six! And do they look like—"

Sin nodded. "All over six feet tall, dark hair, violet eyes, and killer bodies." She laughed at the look of dismay on Maria's face. "Yeah, I know. If they weren't such good guys, it would have been enough to make all the daddies in Tennessee lock up their daughters when they saw the Pendleton boys coming."

"They're all good?" Maria sounded doubtful.

"For the most part," Senada conceded. "If you put aside their chauvinistic overprotectiveness and domineering attitude."

"Ohhhh," Maria purred. "I think I could. Troy is the kind of man I wished I'd met when I was younger. Before I got involved with Rocky's father." She gave a sad forced smile. "How different I was then. Surely I couldn't have ever been that young, that carefree."

Concern washed over Senada. "How is your job at the hotel going?"

"It's okay. I've got enough money saved up for two months' rent. Mrs. Rodriguez takes care of the children and doesn't charge me. So generous, I don't know what to say." She shrugged. "In another month, Rocky will go to school and Angel will start kindergarten. As long as no one gets sick, we might have a shot at staying here." She smiled again, this time more sincerely. "All thanks to Troy."

Senada nodded and looked at the man responsible for her state of emotional upheaval and for Maria's good fortune. He was one of the good guys.

A little later, they left and made sure Senada's new Fudgsicles made it into the freezer. Sin was thinking about what Maria had said.

Troy fiddled with a lock of her hair. "You're quiet."

"Have you noticed that Maria has a crush on you?"

He looked taken aback. "No, she doesn't."

"Yes, she does."

He moved his shoulders as if relieving a muscle cramp. "She told you that?"

Sin laughed. "No, but—"

He shook his head. "There you go. You're jumping to conclusions."

"The woman couldn't keep her eyes off you. She practically drooled on the counter."

When he sighed, she continued. "You're a man. That's why you didn't notice. Men don't really notice when a woman is interested unless they're interested too."

He sifted his hand past her hair to the nape of her neck. "Then how do you explain us?"

"I wouldn't even attempt it."

"Aw, c'mon. Give it a try," he coaxed, pulling her closer.

She felt the tug toward him inside her as much as she did on the outside. Sighing, she wondered what she would eventually do about it. "I really don't know. It's very strange."

He nibbled at her lips. "Strange?"

"Yeah. Strange." She closed her eyes and rubbed her mouth from side to side over his. "You're a good man, Troy. Why don't you go back to Tennessee and get yourself a good girl?"

Troy chuckled low and deep and pulled her against him. "I don't want a good girl, Sin. I want you."

A couple of nights later, they lay in bed. Troy had spent an excruciating amount of time kissing her and undressing her. She tried to pull him closer, but he evaded her.

She sighed in frustration and pleasure. "You are an incredible tease," she said.

"Nah, I just don't like to rush. Too many nice places to stop on the way." He lowered his mouth to her breast and swirled his tongue around and around her nipple.

Budding under his lavish attention, Senada couldn't decide whether to close her eyes or look away. As if he had all the time in the world, he switched his mouth to her other breast and suckled gently. She threaded her fingers through his hair. "Oh, Troy."

He gently twisted one beaded tip as he continued to mouth the other. "You've got such responsive breasts, Sin. I could do this for hours."

Achy arousal stirred inside her. "You do it for hours, and I'll die," she muttered.

He chuckled. "Relax. I'll take care of you."

"You're full of it, Pendleton. You don't want me relaxed. You want me totally crazy. And you do your best to get me there."

"If you weren't so sexy, this wouldn't be half as fun."

"Flattery will get you—" She broke off when he gently bit her, sending her nerve endings into a frenzy.

"I have a question for you," he said, continuing his caresses.

"Ask," she said. *Then please be quiet and make love to me.*

His hand drifted down between her thighs. "Have you thought about getting together with your father again?"

She swallowed, and his fingers slid into the wet secrets of her femininity. "No."

He pulled his hand back slightly. "No?"

She stifled a groan. "No about my father."

"Oh." He touched her intimately again. "Why not?"

"I don't know." Of its own accord, her body arched toward his. She licked her lips. "It was such a disaster."

"Wasn't really well-planned," he said, kissing her lips. "Neutral territory might help too."

"Maybe," she murmured, feeling her mind and body separate. She wasn't paying as much attention to what he was saying as she was to his voice and his hands.

"Would you meet with him again?"

"I don't know. I—" He slipped one of his fingers inside her, and her arousal jumped up the scale.

"So you're not totally against the idea," he continued in a smooth, sensual voice.

"I—uh—" She tugged his head closer and tried to show him the depth of her desire with a long, wicked french kiss.

His quick, short breaths matched hers. He shook his head. "Right?"

Senada knew the time was right for them to make love, felt it. "Right," she agreed.

"Good," he said, and took her mouth again. Minutes later, she called out his name as he took her body, and she took his.

"This is very nice," Senada said to Troy as the maître d' seated them at a table with a crisp white tablecloth, sterling silver, and crystal.

He tugged at his collar, drawing her attention to his tie. The last time she'd seen him wear a real tie was at Lisa and Brick's wedding. "I'm glad you like it. Would you like some wine?" He hesitated. "Can you have wine?"

"A little every now and then. Yes, I believe I'd like some wine tonight." She took a deep breath and caught the scents of fresh-cut flowers and lighted candle on the tabletop along with Continental cuisine.

She glanced at Troy and found his slight uneasiness endearing. "When you said you wanted to take me out for dinner, I didn't expect this."

He gave a wry grin. "The taco grill?"

"Well, perhaps," she admitted, matching his grin with one of her own. "Or the new barbecue place."

"You like it," he said, more clarification than question.

"Yes. You surprised me."

His grin faded. "More to come," he muttered, and the waiter arrived at the table for their beverage order.

More to come. Senada felt a dart of apprehension. She wondered what he meant by that little comment. Why would Troy bring her to an exquisite restaurant thirty miles from town? What was with the suit and tie and slightly nervous manner?

More to come.

If she were a different woman, she might read something into this situation.

The waiter served the wine. Troy lifted his glass and cleared his throat. "I guess now's a good time to tell you why I brought you here."

TEN

A lump formed in Senada's throat. He wasn't *really* going to ask her to ma— She couldn't even think it. "I know the reason. You brought me because the food is supposed to be wonderful."

Troy shook his head. "No, it's more important than food. It's—"

"Atmosphere and service," she interjected nervously. Her heart was pounding. She couldn't let him say this. She didn't know why, but it would ruin everything.

His eyebrows drew together as he viewed her quizzically. "No. This is one of those life-changing—" He broke off and swore. "He's here early. I wanted to prepare you."

"Prepare me?" she asked, perplexed.

Troy swore again. "Your father's coming."

Senada gaped at him. "My father?"

"Yeah." He lowered his voice. "And your, uh, stepmother."

Her stomach felt like lead. She didn't know whether to cry in relief or disappointment. She shook her head. "I—"

"Heads up," he said. "They're right behind you." Troy stood and extended his hand. "How are you, Rex? And Sheree?"

Senada turned her head and felt the room go out of focus. "Daddy," she murmured, then quickly corrected herself and nodded. "Rex. Sheree." She gave Troy a quick glare of displeasure. "What a surprise."

"Surprise?" Rex bellowed. "Pendleton here told me you wanted to see me."

"Of course she does," Troy interjected. "She's just as excited about getting together with you as you were when I called."

Sheree gave a little wince. "How nice. Good evening. Shall we all sit down?"

"Sure, honey," Rex said, helping his wife into a seat. "Did I hear something about you being a farmer from Tennessee?" he asked Troy. "Have you thought about expanding with livestock?"

Senada shut off her listening device and looked over her new stepmother. Troy and Rex went on and on with ranch talk while Senada studied the woman who'd finally captured Rex.

"You gonna tell me, or am I gonna have to

wait forever?" Rex asked her. "Are you ignoring me, Missy, or do you have fuzz in your ears?"

Senada glanced up at him and gave a little shake of her head. "Pardon me, I was just wondering if I'm older than Sheree or not."

Dead silence followed.

Out of the corner of her eye, Senada caught Troy's sigh.

Her father glowered at her. "Now see here, young lady, you—"

Sheree cleared her throat and put her hand over Rex's. "I'm thirty-three."

Senada nodded. "Oh. Not quite twenty years younger than Dad."

Troy groaned. "I need some air," he said, standing. He dragged Senada to her feet. "She does too. Excuse us."

She frowned at him. "I don't want—"

"Yes," he insisted. "You do."

With a firm hand, he led her to the patio in the back of the restaurant. As soon as they walked through the archway, he turned toward her. "Why are you being such a witch?"

Sin looked at him in surprise. "I haven't said hardly anything."

Troy shoved his hands in his pockets and shot her a look of disbelief. "You're making digs about the difference between Sheree's and your father's ages."

"I thought it was a valid question," she said

innocently. "Especially if I'm supposed to call her Mom."

Troy looked up at the ceiling as if he were searching for help. "Oh, Lord."

Sin stepped directly in front of him. "I think I've been extremely reasonable. I didn't tell my father he is still the most insensitive person ever to walk the earth. I didn't ask if he'd knocked up his pretty young wife before the wedding. And I didn't tell you to go to hell for pulling this rotten trick on me."

Troy took a deep breath, and Sin could practically feel him count to ten. "Listen," he said through gritted teeth. "This may be difficult for you to comprehend, since you're so determined to be Ms. Independence until the day you die. But meeting your father tonight and attempting to be nice is for your own good. You don't have any other relatives, Sin. Don't you think you should make a little effort with the *one* you have?"

She resented his interference. It was presumptuous for him to assume he knew what was best for her. Presumptuous, controlling, domineering. She looked at him darkly, thinking she could just walk out and leave him holding the bag. The bag being her father. Troy almost deserved the punishment of her father's company for the next two hours without her to take the heat. Almost. Despite her irritation with him, she suspected he was right. God, how she hated that.

"Quit pouting," he told her.

"I'm not pouting."

"Your bottom lip could catch a baseball."

She sucked in an indignant breath. "You and my father have something in common."

"What's that?" he asked in a wary tone.

"You both need to go to charm school," she told him, and turned away from him.

"Oh, yeah." He snagged her hand and pulled her back around. "Well, it seems to me you've been a little charm-free yourself tonight." He gave her a quick kiss on the lips. "C'mon, Sin, give the guy a chance."

She stared into his eyes. She really liked his honest violet eyes. "Okay. Let's go, but we might want to make dessert to go."

They placed their orders, and Troy was relieved to watch Sin adopt a more gracious attitude. "The ranch looks great," she said to Rex. "You've expanded."

"Every year," he said with a nod. "I'm trying to buy some neighboring property right now."

"Bet your horses are terrific."

Rex cracked a smile. "We still have Brownie."

Troy watched Senada's eyes widen in surprise. "I'm surprised she's still alive."

"Oh, yeah. Kept one of her foals too."

"Brownie?" Troy interjected.

"Sin's favorite horse. Barely a horse really. Small, but this mare has the disposition of a saint."

"I haven't been riding in years," Sin murmured.

"You oughta come out."

A lengthy silence followed where a father's eyes searched his daughter's. Troy saw her soften, just a little. "Thanks. Maybe I will."

The evening continued with small steps forward. Troy and Sheree filled gaps in the conversation. Rex watched Senada.

"I like that dress, Missy. You look pretty in it. Real classy," he said of Senada's simple white sheath.

She grinned. "Thank you, Dad."

"Covers better than that black sleazy thing you wore the other night," he added firmly.

Troy put his hand on Sin's knee and watched Sheree's elbow make contact with Rex's side. Senada's smile tightened slightly. "There's all kinds of tastes for different fashions."

Troy gave her a reassuring squeeze.

Sheree nodded. "That's so true, and in a few months I'll be wearing one kind. Tents."

They all laughed, and the conversation continued. Troy and Rex argued over who would pay the check. After it was paid, Rex turned to Senada with a serious look on his face. "How long have you been sick, baby?"

Sin went very still. Troy felt her body tense, but her tone was casual. "I'm not sick."

"You got the diabetes, don't you?"

"It's a disease, Dad, but I'm not sick," she said patiently. "In fact, I'm probably healthier than I've ever been."

Rex looked unconvinced. He sighed and put his arm around his wife. "Listen, baby, Sheree and I have discussed it, and I want you to know that you can come and live with us if you want to."

Her eyebrows furrowed in confusion. "Why would I want to?"

"Well," he said hesitantly. "In case you ever get sick and can't live alone."

Troy watched Senada's face turn pale. "I'm not going to get sick," she insisted in a painfully precise voice. "If I did, I wouldn't come to you. As I remember, Rex, you don't handle serious illness well."

Rex looked as if he'd been slapped. He stood, and Senada did too, matching his shame with her own indignation.

"It was an offer," he said gruffly. "A father should take care of his daughter."

"And what should a husband do for his wife?" she asked him quietly. "It wasn't an offer. It was penance." She shook her head. "Sorry, Rex, you'll have to find another way to absolve your guilt."

They stood silently for a moment, then her

lips tilted in a sad smile. "We just can't seem to get together without hurting each other, can we, Rex? Sorry if I gave you indigestion." She fluttered her hand toward his, then without touching him, dropped it to her side. "Thanks for dinner. Good night," she murmured, nodding toward Sheree, then walked away.

Troy rose and glanced at Rex with a shrug.

Sin's father waved his hand. "You don't need to say a word. I know it was my mouth as much as it was hers that messed things up. Maybe more," he added. "Go on after her," he said, tilting his head toward the exit. "Maybe she'll calm down once she gets home."

Troy jammed his hands in his pockets as he walked to the front of the restaurant. God, what a mess. And now he was going to have to try to calm Sin down. He glared at a potted plant. He wasn't looking forward to it.

Glancing around the entrance, he didn't see her. He noticed the ladies' room was to the left and concluded she was in there. He sat down in an upholstered chair to wait. A couple of minutes passed, and Rex and Sheree appeared.

Rex frowned. "Where's Sin?"

"I think she's in the restroom," Troy told him.

"Would you like me to check?" Sheree offered.

Troy paused. It *had* been a few minutes. "Yeah, if you don't mind. Thanks."

Sheree smiled and went into the restroom. A minute later she returned, confusion marring her serene features. "No one's in there," she said. "No one at all."

"No one," Troy and Rex said at the same time.

"Well where—"

Rex glanced out the window and swore. "Better take a look."

Troy stared out the window, gaping. He watched as Senada got into the passenger seat of a white convertible. A guy was driving. Troy didn't have a clue who it was. His feet started moving before his brain did.

"What in hell is she—" He nearly pulled the door off the hinges as he opened it. "Sin!" he yelled, but the only response he got was a cloud of exhaust.

Rex walked to his side. "Who was that?"

Troy shook his head. "Don't know."

Rex swore. "She's done it again."

Troy unglued his gaze from the license plate of the white convertible. "What do you mean, she's done it again?"

"Run off," Rex said with a sigh. "She used to do this all the time when she was a teenager. Especially when she was upset."

Run off. Troy felt a sinking sensation. He was responsible for this. "Where'd she go?"

"Usually somewhere just over the border in Mexico."

He resisted the urge to swear. "Anywhere in particular?" he asked, knowing he was going to have to go get her.

Rex made a clicking noise with his tongue and shook his head. "I can give you a few suggestions, but Mexico's got more little border places than I've got cattle. And I've got a lot of cattle, Troy."

"Give me the short list."

"It'll be like looking for a needle in a haystack," Rex warned.

"I don't have a choice," Troy told the older man. "She's upset. I'm partly responsible."

Troy quickly learned he was at a disadvantage. The Mexicans he encountered found it extremely amusing that he was looking for a woman. *"Muchas muchachas bonitas."*

He went into bars asking the same question. At the eleventh, a young English-speaking man overheard his conversation with the bartender and approached him. "You looking for the one they call Sin?"

Troy gave the guy a double take. "Yeah. You know where she is?"

"She was here earlier." The guy motioned the bartender for another beer. "About an hour."

Troy ground his teeth. "Do you know where she was headed?"

The man gave Troy a look of sympathy. "Sorry. I just heard her say she wanted to dance."

"Dance," Troy echoed. He was going to kill her. When he found her. "You mind giving me a short list of the most popular places for *dancing*?"

The man obliged, and Troy continued his quest. He stopped in one place and would have sworn he could smell her perfume. She was nowhere to be seen, however, so he went on.

The next to the last bar was a loud, jumping place. The music was fast and hot, the crowd of people spilling out onto the porch, and the walls of the building seemed to bulge and vibrate from the pounding rhythm of drums and feet. Hoots and rippling screams of delight echoed out the open windows.

Sin was there.

Troy knew it, felt it in his bones, and he steeled himself for seeing her as he climbed the steps. He walked through the door and took a moment for his eyes to adjust. The room was a mass of gyrating bodies, and the smell of Mexican beer and tequila was strong. As soon as his gaze focused, he saw her. She would have been hard to miss.

Since she was dancing on a tabletop with a half-dozen men cheering her on.

Troy swore and moved toward her. Thank the Lord for small things, he told himself. At least she was still fully dressed. The way she moved, however, compensated for her conservative nice-girl sheath. Her hands lifted on either side of her body, she twisted and swiveled, alternately tiptoeing and stomping her heels on the wooden tabletop. Her hair was wild and loose. Any man would want to sift his fingers through it and get lost. Any man would want those silky waves flowing over his body.

As did the men at her feet.

Troy gave a wry chuckle. Sin was so accustomed to having men at her feet, she didn't seem to notice them. She danced unto herself, passionate, her eyes staring off into the distance as she spent her energy and emotion. She smiled at no one in particular, clearly enjoying the music.

It was cathartic, he realized, and his urge to wring her neck died a quick death. Dinner had been too much, and this was her way of venting. "Well, hell," he muttered. He'd been afraid she was going to do something to hurt herself.

Instead she just needed to let off a little steam.

The song ended and the crowd screamed for more. Sin paused, but when the music began again, so did she. Troy grabbed a chair off to the side and checked his watch. Midnight. He let out a sigh and shifted to get comfortable. He unbuttoned a couple of shirt buttons, thankful he'd ditched his coat and tie earlier. He might as well settle in.

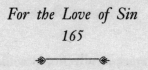

Senada felt her stomach rumble and knew it was time to eat. She had a pack of crackers in her purse that would keep her in balance, but she'd danced for hours and, wonder of wonders, her feet were starting to hurt.

"Must be getting old," she muttered, glancing down at her high heels. She felt tired, but better. The music lifted her spirit, dancing took the edge off her disappointing meeting with her father, and now she'd be able to sleep like a baby.

As long as she found a ride home. Ricardo, the man fate had brought by the restaurant at just the right moment, had consumed a little too much tequila. Unfortunately, when Ricardo drank too much tequila he became convinced that he was God's gift to women and that no woman could resist him.

She sighed. That could be tiresome right now. Glancing down at the men standing around her table, she smiled. "It's been fun, boys, but it's time for me to go. Where's the phone?"

They moaned their disappointment and made various amorous suggestions in Spanish and English. She smiled again and shook her head. "You tempt me, but you're all so wonderful. I can only handle one man at a time. How could I choose?"

More suggestions followed while she looked toward the bar for the phone. Spotting it, she stepped down from the table onto a chair. One of the men was determined to assist her, putting his hand at her waist and taking her hand. She murmured a quick "*Gracias,*" and extricated herself. It took another little dance, but she escaped and arrived at the phone, purse in hand. She dialed for a taxi and waited while the dispatcher took his time.

When he told her no cabs were available, she bit back an oath of frustration. "What do you mean you only have two drivers working tonight and both are busy?" she demanded.

From behind her, a large masculine hand pushed the receiver down, and Sin whipped around to tear a strip off the macho idiot who dared—

She stopped dead when she saw it was Troy. "You've had a busy night, haven't you?"

She hadn't expected him. The mere sight of him, his presence, grabbed at her heart. God, he looked good to her.

He raised his eyebrows at her silence. "Need a ride?"

She stared into his eyes expecting censure, but finding none. She waited a moment, wondering when he was going to start in on how irresponsible she'd been. He didn't. In fact, he seemed at ease, accepting.

"Or did you want to dance some more?" he added.

She shook her head, still unsure of him. "No. I'd like to go home."

"I can do that."

She walked with him out to the car and got in. It was on the tip of her tongue to ask him how he'd found her. Senada bit her tongue. Taking an inventory of his appearance, she wondered what was going through his mind. He wore the shirt and slacks from dinner, but he looked rumpled in a sexy, masculine way. His hair was mussed as if he'd run his hand through it several times in exasperation. Senada restrained the urge to smile. Her middle name was exasperation.

He started the engine and pulled onto the road. "Didn't know you were such a good dancer," he said.

She felt a dart of surprising selfconsciousness. "You saw me."

"Kinda hard to miss," he said. "I watched the last thirty-minute set. The guys around your table looked entertained."

"You should have joined them," she told him, giving it back to him a little.

"Never was much for being one of a crowd."

"You'd prefer a private dance?" She heard the huskiness in her voice and wondered where it had come from.

A charged silence followed before he dipped

his head. "Is that an offer?" he asked low and deep.

She felt a wicked surge of excitement. "Guess you'll have to find out."

He chuckled. "You're a tease, Sin. You could drive a man insane."

Satisfied he might not grill her after all, she relaxed and laid her head back on the seat. "I think insanity's underrated. Look at all the things you can get away with if people think you're insane. You can dress however you like, walk in the rain without an umbrella, sing in public, dance at a funeral—"

"Dance on top of a table in a Mexican tavern with six men salivating at your feet," Troy interjected.

Sin smiled. "You think they were interested in my feet?"

Troy sighed. "I think they were interested in every inch of you."

"Some inches more than others."

"Are you trying to provoke me?"

"Yes. It's one of my little hobbies."

"Thought of another benefit to insanity, Sin."

She turned her head toward him, admiring his strong profile. "Oh, yeah?"

He nodded, a mock warning glint in his eye. "People use it to get away with murder."

ELEVEN

Sin slept on the drive home, and Troy expected he would carry her inside. Instead she woke just as he cut the engine. Yawning, she stretched, then blinked her eyes. She looked at Troy and smiled. "Thanks for the ride. Coming in?"

He nodded, unwilling to quibble with her casual invitation. Earlier in the evening, he'd wondered if she would speak to him again, let alone invite him back into her home.

They walked up the walk and inside the house. She dropped her purse on a table in the living room. "Bet you're tired, aren't you?"

He rubbed the back of his neck. "A little."

"Have a seat," she said. "I'll get us something to drink."

Shrugging, he sank onto the sofa and turned his head from side to side to relieve the tension in his neck. She returned with wine for him and water for her. She was eating an apple. Slipping past him, she put a CD in her stereo, then joined him on the sofa.

She ate a few more bites of the apple and, feeling his gaze on her, stopped. She looked at the apple, then at him. "Want a bite?"

Troy felt his stomach tighten. The woman didn't have a clue. He wanted whatever she offered him and more. "Yeah, I do," he said, and lifted the hand she used to hold the apple to his mouth. The fruit was juicy and sweet with just a hint of tartness. *Like Sin.* Troy kept his thoughts to himself.

"How did you find me?" she asked.

Troy thought back to the number of bars he'd gone through and took a drink of his wine. "Lists," he said.

"Lists?" she echoed, her eyes mirroring her confusion.

"Your father said you'd probably gone over the border, and I asked him for a list of possible places."

"Oh," she said in a small voice. "How, uh, long was this list?"

"He gave me the name of a dozen places."

Senada winced.

Troy took another drink. "I only went to eleven."

"Oh," she said again, clearly unsure how to respond.

He was starting to enjoy this. "At the eleventh place, I ran into a guy who had seen you. He'd overheard you say you wanted to dance. He gave me the second list."

Senada's face fell. "The second list?"

"Yeah. This one was for the most popular places people go to dance. You were at the third one."

She stared at him in disbelief. "You went to fourteen different places looking for me."

Troy nodded and chuckled. "I'm a persistent sonovabitch."

Her eyes were filled with wonder. "No one has ever gone to that much trouble for me. Ever."

Troy felt his grin fade. He'd never loved a woman the way he loved Sin either, but he wasn't ready to say the words aloud. She wasn't ready to hear them either, he thought. The moment wrapped around them like a tight rubber-band, binding them together.

Senada leaned closer, her gaze searching his. "Wanna dance?"

Dance? Troy heard the warm huskiness in her tone and wondered if he'd ever make sense of her. "It's two A.M."

She gave a slow smile. "Early."

"You have to work tomorrow."

Sin stood. "This is your offer for a private dance. Are you going to shut up and dance with me or not?"

Troy, who had a retort for nearly everything, clamped his mouth shut and joined her.

He hadn't paid any attention to the music until now. A female singer with a plaintive, ethereal voice wove a little magic inside him, making his protected, buried feelings rise to the surface. The music made him feel vulnerable. He was unaccustomed to the sensation and might have fought it, but the woman who had stolen his heart was in his arms.

She led him. He led her. She put her hand on his chest where his heart beat, and with her gaze meeting his, she brushed away his shirt.

Unable to wait any longer, he kissed her long with naked emotion. She kindled his need with her response.

"Do you want me?" he asked.

"Yes." She opened her mouth against his neck and pulled him closer.

"Show me," he whispered.

And with the music winding its spell around them, she did, with every touch, every caress, every private pleasure. When his clothes were gone and hers were too, they still danced, nude, her warm, moist body undulating against his hard hungry form. He wanted her so much he hurt. It was more than a physical pain. It went all the way to his well-guarded heart.

When the arousal became too much, he pulled her down to the carpet with him, kissing her and fondling her. The passion in her eyes made him mindless. They tussled, and this time she ended up on top. The sight of her, her breasts full from his touch, her nipples shiny from his lips, and her wanton mouth swollen from their kisses, made him arch toward her as she hovered over him.

She sank onto him, taking him all the way in. For a moment, he couldn't breathe. "Sin?" he asked when his body was completely enveloped by her tight wet velvet.

She licked her lips and sighed in pleasure. "Yes," she whispered.

"Have you ever loved one of your lovers?" It was the damnedest thing, but he needed to know he was different.

She bit her lip and looked at him. For once, it was as if she was letting him see all her secrets, all her dreams, all her emotions. She leaned forward until her mouth glanced his, and he tried not to be disappointed that she hadn't answered.

Then she whispered, "Not before you."

Senada slapped blindly at her alarm clock this morning. She really didn't want to get up. After she and Troy had made love the night before, they'd gone back and forth about which one was going to carry the other to bed. They ended up supporting each other and falling onto the mattress.

She sighed. She really didn't want to get up.

But that damned needle was waiting for her.

Pulling her way to the side of the bed, she slid one foot onto the floor. At the same time, the long arm of Troy slid across her waist.

"Going somewhere?" he mumbled.

Senada smiled. "Yes. To the bathroom."

"Can I come?"

She chuckled. "No." She slid her other foot on the floor and stood.

Troy pulled himself up on his elbow. Senada stared at him for a long moment. His brilliant eyes were heavy lidded, his eyelashes a sexy shield. His hair was mussed, his jaw dark with a morning-after shadow, and since he'd kicked the sheets aside, his heaven-help-me body was unselfconsciously bare to her gaze.

She shook her head. "I tell you one thing, Pendleton, you are one gorgeous man."

His gaze slid over her in heated approval. "You're not too bad yourself, Sin. Come back to bed."

The invitation gave her a rush of excitement. "In a minute. I've got—" she winced, "a date with a needle."

He started to rise. "Let me watch."

She held out her hand. "No! Really, no."

Exasperation crossed his face. "I've seen every square inch of your body, Sin, up close and personal. And you won't let me watch you give yourself an injection."

Sin grabbed her robe and shook her head. "A

woman likes to keep a little mystery," she told him, but she noticed he didn't smile.

Troy arrived at the bar later than usual that night. Giving an absent wave to someone who called his name, he sat down at a table and ordered a beer. He'd just finished a heated discussion with his brother Brick. Brick was insistent about learning the mystery of why Sin had left Tennessee. Now that Troy knew everything, however, he was struggling with an odd reluctance to reveal Sin's condition.

He swore. The woman was going to drive him crazy. Brick had also informed him that Daniel needed him at the farm as soon as he could manage it. Technically, Troy should be ready to go. His job was done. With all he'd learned about Sin, though, he was stuck with the feeling of an uncompleted task. Troy hated that. He'd never been afraid of a problem, because he'd always believed he could find the solution. He suspected part of the solution for Sin was settling up with her father; and successfully getting those two together would probably require the services of a professional engineer and a psychologist. Troy was neither.

"You're glowering," Sin said, interrupting his thoughts as she looked down at him. "In a bad mood?"

"I talked to Brick."

She gave a laugh. "Oh, well, that'll put you in a bad mood."

"No," he said. "He and Daniel are chewing on me, but I've got some other things on my mind. Did you hear about Maria?"

She shook her head and sat next to him. "What?"

"She lost her job at the motel."

"Oh, no. What happened?"

"Her little girl got sick. Maria had to go in late. They fired her." Troy sighed. "I'm trying to think of a job for her, but I don't know this area."

"I'd hire her here, but the hours are terrible for someone with kids."

Troy shrugged. "Maybe you can ask around."

"I will." She took his hand in hers. "If it's broke, you've got to try to fix it, don't you?"

He liked the feel of her fingers wrapped around his. "Hadn't really thought about it that way, but maybe I do." He cleared his throat. "Which brings up another subject. Did you ever call your father back?" Rex had called while Sin was taking a shower.

She tried to pull her hand away, but he wouldn't allow it. "I didn't have time."

"He's worried about you."

"He shouldn't be. I'm fine."

"I think he wants to apologize for last night."

"Oh, save me." Senada laughed. "You don't know Rex. Even when he apologizes, he somehow makes it seem as if I'm responsible."

Troy rubbed his jaw. "Maybe he's changed."

Senada shot him a doubtful look. "Not that I can see."

He tugged at her hand and held her gaze. "But you've changed. You're not seventeen, anymore. It might be time for you to be the leader."

That stopped her. She thought about it. He could see the wheels turning, then a waitress called her name. She leaned closer and gave him a quick kiss. "If you really want to fix something," she said in a sexy voice, "the ice maker's broken again."

He swatted her on the behind as she left and sighed. How was he going to go back to Tennessee without her?

He brooded over that the rest of the night and checked on Sin throughout the evening. He kept remembering when she went into insulin shock, and the possibility that it could happen again scared the spit out of him.

"I haven't seen you eat anything in a while," he said around midnight when she was pouring two pitchers of beer.

She glanced at her watch and made a moue of surprise. "I'm going to snitch something in a few minutes. It's been busy tonight, hasn't it?" She set the pitchers on a tray and handed them to a waitress.

He didn't like the circles he saw under her eyes. "You look tired."

She tossed him a suggestive smile as she grabbed a cloth to wipe the bar. "I had a very active night last night."

"You should have rested more today," he grumbled. "Did you take your insulin when you were supposed to?"

Senada sighed and turned away. "You know, Troy, sometimes you can be a real killjoy."

"Does that mean you haven't?"

She turned back toward him. "No. It means I don't want to discuss it with you." She lowered her voice. "I'm in charge of my insulin. Okay? Diabetes is a fact of life for me, but I don't like being made to feel like an invalid."

"It was that reaction you had at your father's ranch. You didn't see how pale you were, how lethargic."

Sin had her own feelings about that experience. It had been plenty scary for her. "If it will make you feel any better," she told him, "I didn't enjoy feeling that way, and I'm going to do everything I can to make sure I don't repeat the experience." She paused, looking into his eyes and feeling the undertow of her uncertainty about her disease. She fought that undertow every day.

"The truth is, Troy, it will probably happen again. Sometime, someday, I won't do something I was supposed to because I'm not perfect, and it might happen again. I have to live with that, but I'm not your responsibility, so you don't need to worry about it. I'm making sure nobody feels responsible."

Troy looked at her as if she'd slapped him.

Confused, she tugged gently at his sleeve and tried for a smile. "You're supposed to be relieved, unburdened," she said. "I don't expect you to take care of me. That's supposed to make you feel better."

His eyes darkened and he backed away. "Yeah. Sure."

That night, he made love to her again and again throughout the night. When morning came, he didn't ask if he could watch her give herself her injection. He'd learned, ironically enough, that while Sin might give him her body, she would never afford him every intimacy. The knowledge lashed at him.

Troy brushed aside that issue in favor of making some headway about her father. "He wants you to come to the ranch today," Troy told her after breakfast.

"It's not a good day for me. I'm busy," she said as she cleared the table.

Troy followed her into the kitchen. "He's expecting you."

She did a double take. "Expecting me? Is this

a royal command?" She gave a short laugh. "That doesn't work with me, anymore."

Troy braced himself. She was *not* going to be happy with what he had done. "I told him you'd come."

She dropped a dish in the sink and stared at him. "You did what?"

"I told him you'd come."

Fury lit her eyes. "Well, you can just untell him."

Troy stood his ground. "No."

She blinked. "I think we're having a communication problem." She shook her head. "I'm not going to see my father today."

"I think you should," he said calmly. "I think he's really going to try to be reasonable this time."

"*You* think I should," she repeated, looking like a firecracker ready to go off. "*You* think he'll be reasonable." She looked at the glass she was holding as if she wanted to break it. Instead, she set it down, none too gently. "You've gone too far this time, Troy. This is none of your business." She started to walk from the room.

"I did it because I love you."

She stopped midstride. He watched a dozen emotions come and go in her eyes, surprise and hope, then doubt and suspicion. She took a deep breath and continued into the dining room to pick up the rest of the dishes. "If you'd said that at a different time, I might have been delighted.

Unfortunately, I've learned that people pull out that little three-word phrase at the darndest moments, like when they want you to do something you don't want to do."

Something inside him splintered. "I told you before, you've been hanging around the wrong kind of men."

"Well one of those men who taught me so well was my father," she retorted, tossing the plate into the sink with such force that it broke. Sin stared at it and swore under her breath. She sighed and shook her head.

Troy heard the wealth of hurt in her revealing statement. He pushed his hand through his hair in exasperation.

"I hate to be the one to tell you this, Troy, to wreck your idealistic beliefs. But you can't fix everything." She stood in front of him and met his gaze. "You can't fix my relationship with my father unless we want it fixed. And right now we obviously don't."

She took a breath and went on. "You can't fix my diabetes. It won't go away. I hate it that I got this. Absolutely hate it. I hate the adjustments I've had to make. Hate the needles. Hate the diet. Hate the extra risks and the fact that I've got to be careful about things other people don't have to think twice about. Like stubbing a toe. If I ever get married, my husband will have to deal with the possibilities, and not all of them are pretty. If I ever decide to get pregnant, there will be extra considerations."

She lifted her hands. Her voice was calm, but her eyes said she'd had it. "You're a nice guy, Troy, but I've got to settle this one on my own, and I don't have it all taken care of yet. So, until I do, just leave me the hell alone."

She walked toward her bedroom, calling over her shoulder, "I'm going out for a while."

Troy stared after her. Within minutes, she was whipping past him with her car keys, then slamming the front door behind her. A heavy sense of dread filled his gut. Sin was right. He'd gone too far, stepped over the line.

It was time to go.

She drove for an hour. It was too hot, but she rolled down the window anyway. She wanted to feel the wind in her hair, and closing the windows trapped her inside her little car with all her big feelings and busy thoughts.

One thing she hated, yet secretly liked about Troy Pendleton, was that he made her face the truth. He didn't sugarcoat it, didn't try to paint it a pretty color, but he also didn't let her evade it.

She hadn't made any of those statements about diabetes aloud until Troy pushed the issue. It was crazy, but saying them aloud took a big bite out of her fear. She remembered how her dietician had encouraged her to attend the support group meetings, and the light began to dawn. She wondered, for a moment, though, if saying it to someone who loved you made a difference.

Troy Pendleton had stomped into her life and turned it upside down. Before, she'd resented him.

Now, she was grateful.

Stop fooling yourself.

Her heart twisted. She swore. She hadn't expected this. Was unprepared for her feelings. But she wasn't just grateful. She was in love.

She was so rattled by the realization that she almost didn't notice what road she was on. Sin saw the familiar signs and realized her father's ranch was just beyond the next curve.

She laughed at the irony. It was as if Troy had driven her there himself.

TWELVE

Senada sat down on the brocade sofa in the formal living room. The sofa didn't hold happy memories, considering the last time she reclined on it she'd had a reaction to her insulin. She remembered her father bellowing in the background.

"You're here early," Rex said as he stomped into the room.

Senada smiled wryly and stood. "Last time I was late. This time, I'm early. We have a tough time coordinating our timetables, don't we?"

Looking slightly taken aback, he stared at her for a moment, then cleared his throat. "I guess we do."

"Can we go for a ride?" she asked.

Surprise crossed his face again. "Well, uh—"

"We haven't been in a long time."

His hard features softened. "That we

haven't." He looked her over. "You sure you want to wear those tennis shoes? Let me see if Sheree has some boots that'll fit you."

Minutes later, they saddled up and were riding toward the west pasture. Sin was impressed with the improvements he'd made in the ranch. "You've worked hard and it shows."

He glanced over at her. "I've had a lot of time to kill. Figured I might as well do something constructive."

Sin allowed herself to settle into the mare's rolling gait. "I always thought of you as busy, not killing time."

He gave a humorless chuckle. "After your mom died, I was killing time. I knew I'd screwed up the best thing in my life when I abandoned you two, but I didn't think I could handle a slow good-bye. I thought quick would be better. Hadn't counted on the guilt."

Sin stared at him in shock. Rex had *never* admitted guilt before.

"What's the matter, Sin? Cat got your tongue? You look a little surprised."

She caught her breath. "Well, I guess I am. Whenever I brought up the way Mom died, you blew me off."

"Because you were usually screaming about what a rotten husband, father, and human being I was."

"I did n—" She stopped herself, her memory clicking in. As a teenager she'd taken every opportunity to remind Rex of his failings. "I guess I did," she admitted.

Rex pulled his gelding to a stop and looked at her. "Senada, what I did to you and your mama was wrong, and there hasn't been a day that passed that I didn't regret it. I didn't just lose the only woman I've ever really loved. I lost my baby girl too." A lump formed in her throat.

"Why did you do it? Why did you walk away?"

Rex sucked in a deep breath. "I couldn't handle it. Couldn't handle watching her go down. I started drinking and wrecked the car one night. Ran into a tree. It was a wonder I didn't kill myself or somebody else. That's when I knew I couldn't keep watching her die. It's a damned helpless feeling to watch your wife die knowing you can't do a thing to stop it." He tilted his hat backward. "Figured there'd better be a place for you to call home after your mom was gone, so I put my energy into that."

Seneda's heart felt like it was breaking. She'd felt those same feelings of helplessness. Her eyes began to burn. "I was really grateful, wasn't I?"

Rex shook his head. "No. You were a handful. I thought about tearing out both your hair and mine more than a few times. I kept hoping you'd stop resenting me." He smiled sadly. "Kept hoping you'd forgive me."

"I didn't want to forgive you," she whispered as much to herself as to him. "It was easier to be angry. I didn't have to think about the loss if I resented you."

Silence followed. The truth hit her hard. Senada held her breath for a long moment coming to grips with it. Myriad thoughts and feelings swam inside her. Her hands were shaking. Had she *really* hung on to her resentment all those years to avoid the hurt?

She finally took a careful breath. "We really made a mess of things, didn't we?"

Rex was watching her carefully. "Yeah, we did."

"I hated the women," she told him.

"Hell, I must've gone through a dozen. It was like trying to plug a hole in a ship. Just kept getting bigger." He met her gaze. "I can't go back and change any of this."

"Neither of us can."

Rex nodded silently in understanding while his gelding shifted beneath him as if he was bored from standing. It was odd, Senada thought, how a quiet understanding passed between them.

Another thought persisted, though, and she had to voice it. "When I was diagnosed, I quit my partnership in Tennessee and came here. In the back of my mind, I was running home, but when I got here I was afraid to tell you. Afraid you'd turn away like before."

Rex's face wrinkled in agony. He shook his

head. "It won't happen, Senada. I swear it, baby. I ran away from your mother, and I've been paying for it ever since." He looked down, then back at her. "Hate to admit this, but sometimes it takes a long time for a man to become a man."

And Rex had become a man. She could see it. It might be hard for him, but she knew he would stay with her even if it killed him. The dam of resentment burst inside her, and the feeling of freedom and hope made her dizzy. She blinked at tears blurring her vision. Her throat was knotted, her chest tight, and she was ready to sob. "Oh, Daddy, you think we can turn this thing around now after all these years?"

Before she knew it, he was beside her, pulling her down and holding her in his arms as if she were ten again. "I've been dreaming of this day for years. I almost can't believe it's true."

"Me too." She swallowed hard and thought of Troy. How had he known? She patted her father on the back. "There's someone I need to thank."

"Later," Rex said. "We've got some catching up to do."

Hours later, Sin arrived back at her house, feeling exhausted and elated. She and her father had talked and talked. They'd argued about a few things, but it had been good-natured. He wanted her to move into his house. She told him to forget it. "I want us to stay on speaking terms for longer than twenty-four hours," she'd said.

He'd grumbled, but relented. He'd also been anxious about her diagnosis. After she'd filled him in on her treatment, he seemed to relax a little. He would keep a watchful eye, though, she thought. And she didn't mind it. She even kind of liked it.

Troy's rental car was missing, so he must have gone out, she decided. She needed to apologize. She needed to thank him. And then she needed to tell him that she loved him. The thought terrified her, but she wanted to do it. She wanted him to know.

She headed for the kitchen to clean up the mess she'd made and stopped when she saw the plate she'd broken on the kitchen counter. It had been glued back together, and there was a note attached.

Senada,
I'm not sure it's usable, but it's fixed. I couldn't resist trying. Sorry if I made things more difficult for you. I understand you need to make your own way. If you ever decide you want to share your life with others, remember there are people in Tennessee who love you.
Take care,
Troy

Senada stared at the note and felt her heart fall to her feet. She reread it again and again. No hidden messages. No questions. No frills. The message was clear.

Troy was gone. She'd waited too long.

She went through the motions of her routine, went to work, ate when she was supposed to, and took her insulin. She even went to bed at her regular time.

But she couldn't sleep.

Troy's scent was still in the room. It was too easy to imagine his body right next to hers as it had been the night before. Too easy to remember the sound of his voice, low and sexy. Too easy to recall the way his breath drifted over her hair and his hand wrapped around her waist, pulling her against him.

So easy and so hard.

Sin sat up in bed and flicked on the beside light. She needed to shoo his ghost away. With the light on, she *knew* he wasn't there. Yet, his scent remained.

Swearing, she got up from her bed, took a freshly laundered blanket from the linen closet, and made her way to the living room sofa. It took another hour of telling herself not to think about him before she finally fell asleep, and when she did, she dreamed about him.

The next morning, she changed the sheets, laundered the bedspread, and lit a candle to purge his scent and presence from the room.

When she went to bed that night, however, she still couldn't sleep. Dozing on the couch became a ritual that lasted for five nights.

Cranky and bemused, she unloaded on her dietician at her regular appointment. "I have *always* been the one to finish a relationship, Helen."

Helen nodded. "So this is ego?"

Senada paused. "Ego," she repeated, and laughed. "I wish."

Helen's eyebrows rose. "Oh, my. I take it you'd like an on-going relationship with this man."

Sin nodded. "Yes. But it will be difficult with him in Tennessee and me in Texas. Plus, there's the fact that he left and he hasn't called."

"True," Helen said, and continued to pencil in some foods for Senada on her menu. "The distance between Tennessee and Texas might as well be the same as the North Pole and the South Pole."

Sin started to nod, then stopped. "It's not quite that far."

"Hmmm. And the reason he hasn't called probably doesn't have anything to do with your obsession to remain independent."

Indignation flared inside her. "I'm not obsessed."

Helen gazed at her skeptically. "Hmmm."

"I'm not obsessed," Sin insisted. "Look at how my father and I have made amends. I even asked him to give my neighbor a job. I've been to dinner at his house twice since our big pow-wow."

"So why are you so upset about Troy?"

Senada's heart squeezed tight. "I didn't want him to go," she admitted. "I liked being with him. Other men I get tired of after a few hours of their nonstop company. But I even like bickering with Troy. I was really surprised when I found out he wasn't as dumb as I thought he was."

Helen shook her head. "You didn't give him that last overwhelming compliment, did you?"

"No, but I thought it." She stood and paced around the small office. "And I really liked the attention he paid to me. I mean, I know my body turned him on, but he was always trying to get past what I said to what I really *meant*. Being with him got to be a habit," she said, and the knowledge hurt. "And I don't want to break the habit."

Helen sat back in her seat. "Do you think he loves you?"

Her insides twisted and splintered. She wondered how she could feel euphoric and sad at the same time. "Yes," she said quietly. "I think he does." What a revelation, she thought. Even though he'd said it, even though he'd acted it, it had taken him leaving for her to comprehend the truth.

Helen shrugged. "Then it seems to me your decision is easy. Are you going to fly or drive?"

Sin ended up driving a week later.

She didn't just drive herself. With help from one of her father's ranch hands, she loaded a trailer with most of her worldly possessions. She quit her job, got out of her lease, and after a long talk with Rex, headed north.

The hours of riding afforded her several opportunities to reconsider, to come to her senses, and turn back, but Sin kept on going. She'd gotten what she came for in Texas, and now it was time to go back to the people who loved her. Though she could tell her departure saddened her father, she knew their relationship would never be distant again.

After pulling into a Chattanooga hotel just after noon, she freshened up and called Lisa, who insisted Sin come over immediately.

"You're back! You're back!" Lisa said, a baby on her hip, as she opened the front door to her traditional home. Her face scrubbed free of makeup, her light brown hair tied up in ponytail, and dressed in casual shorts that accented her long, lean figure, she looked happier than ever. "Come here," she said, and hugged Sin.

Sin returned Lisa's embrace and smiled at the youngster. "She's adorable. Got your face and the Pendleton eyes."

"Brick's chin," Lisa corrected with a grimace. "Stubborn. All three of them got Brick's chin."

"Where is the iron man?" Sin asked.

Lisa grinned at the familiar joke between them. Sin often deliberately *forgot* Brick's name. "Brick, Sin. Not rock, not iron, or steel. Brick." She rolled her eyes and led Senada to the family room, where the other two babies lay in the playpen. "You *are* staying for dinner, aren't you? He'll be crushed if he misses you."

"I bet," Sin said wryly, knowing Brick had very mixed feelings about her. She sat down on the couch.

"No," Lisa said, shifting the child. "Really. He wants to grill you about Troy."

Sin's heart caught. "Why?"

"Because ever since Troy came back from Texas, he's been quiet." Lisa met Senada's gaze squarely. "Quiet," she repeated. "Troy is many things, but quiet isn't one of them."

"Oh," Sin murmured, wondering what the quiet meant. "He told you why I went to Texas, didn't he?"

"No. He said it was your business. Your place to tell or not tell."

Sin gaped at her longtime friend. She put her hand to her throat in surprise. "I—uh—" She shook her head. "He didn't tell you I was diagnosed with diabetes?"

Now it was Lisa's turn to look shocked. "No." Her pretty face wrinkled in concern.

"Are you okay? That must have been frightening. How long has it—" She stopped and looked at Sin with hurt indignation. "Why didn't you tell me!"

Sin stood. "It's a long story," she began.

"I've got all afternoon," Lisa insisted.

Sin gave Lisa the background on her diagnosis and her mother's death. While she told her friend, she felt foolish for turning away from her close friends when she'd been hurting. She was relieved that Lisa didn't blame her and was just pleased to have Sin back in town. Lisa wanted to make plans to put their catering business back together as soon as Sin could manage it. The two were discussing clients when Brick walked through the door.

Followed by Troy.

"Hi, honey, I dragged my mute brother along for dinner since—" Brick, the biggest of the Pendleton brothers, broke off when he saw Sin. Distrust and reluctant affection warred in his gaze. "Well, well, look what the wind blew in."

Lisa fluttered to her feet. "Sweetheart, Sin's just been telling me . . ."

Sin knew Lisa was talking, but she couldn't have repeated a word. She was too busy staring at Troy. She was so immobilized, she wondered how she managed to breathe. Inside, she was sweating and swearing. She wasn't prepared for this. She'd wanted to take a shower first, compose herself, practice in front of a mirror.

She gave herself a hard mental shake. She was Senada Calhoun. Cool, in control, she could reduce most men to stuttering. She held all the cards in a relationship. She said when. She said how. She said good-bye.

At that moment, she couldn't form the word *boo*. And she was about as mighty as Jell-O.

Suddenly, Lisa stopped talking, and she and Brick were alternately staring at Sin and Troy.

Holding her gaze, Troy nodded. "It's good to see you, Sin. You doing okay?"

She cleared her throat. "Yes."

"Good," he muttered, and looked away.

She waited for him to say something else, but he didn't. Lisa gazed at him searchingly and began to fill the silence. "Sin's had a long drive, so I thought we'd go ahead with dinner and . . ."

Brick gave Lisa a kiss and squeezed her against him, then picked up two of his babies. Troy took the one Lisa held, and within minutes they all sat around the kitchen table.

"Where are you staying, anyway?" Lisa asked as they began to eat.

"A hotel for now," Sin said, ever conscious of Troy's presence. *Why wasn't he saying anything?*

"We've got an extra room," Lisa said.

Brick blanched.

Senada laughed. "That's okay. I've got a

trailer, so I'll need to make a quick decision about where I'm going to live."

"Live," Brick echoed, glancing at Troy. "So you're really back?"

"Yes. I am." She looked for Troy's response, but when there was none, she felt a sinking sensation in her stomach. Perhaps she'd overestimated his feelings for her.

Troy played with his triplet nieces and remained quiet the rest of the evening. Senada grew distressed. Concerned that she would be unable to hide her feelings, she decided to leave. She thanked Brick and Lisa, tickled the three little girls under their fat little chins, and gave a quick nod to Troy.

"G'night."

He finally met her gaze. "Glad you're back, Sin, for however long you decide to stay."

Senada paused, taking in his statement. It told her everything. He was afraid she was going to leave. "I'm here to stay, Troy," she told him, feeling a smile climb out from inside her. "For good." Because she just couldn't resist, she lowered her voice to a purr. "Come by room four-thirty-three at my hotel tomorrow at seven A.M. if you want to see something you've never seen before."

Then she walked out the door and let Mr. No-Talk chew on that for a while.

At three minutes till seven, Troy rapped on Senada's door. Ever since he left Sin, he'd had to do everything but break his fingers to keep from calling her. He felt as if he'd gone through a meat grinder, and it was all he could do to put a good face on every day. His brothers were nagging the living daylights out of him.

He hadn't counted on falling in love with the modern-day equivalent of Mata Hari. He swore under his breath. How the hell was he supposed to find a way to get her to stay with him? He swore again.

Sin opened the door and stared at him, her brown eyes wide with emotion and questions. "Come on in," she murmured.

Her hair was damp from her shower, and she wore the silk robe he'd taken off of her so many times. "A lot has happened since I last saw you," she said, heading for the bathroom. "I went for a ride with my dad, and we're speaking again. I have you to thank for that." She met his gaze. "Thank you."

Speechless, Troy stood outside the bathroom. "I didn't do any—"

"Yes, you did. You knew better than either of us did how much my dad and I needed to reconcile our differences."

He shrugged, still bowled over by her gratitude. "Okay."

She stepped inside the bathroom and gazed

at him expectantly. "Well, are you coming or not?"

Confused, he stared at her. He'd always known Sin was a little sideways, but this was— She lifted a syringe. His internal protests died and he stepped inside.

She gave a tight smile. "Get ready for the greatest show on earth."

His heart flipped over. "Sin, you don't have to—"

"Yes. I do." She bit her lip. "Sorry the accommodations are a little tight, but this won't take long. You want to sit on the side of the tub? Don't worry. I dried it off."

She pulled out an alcohol pad and tore it open. "I talked Rex into giving Maria a job. She and the kids are moving to the ranch."

She looked matter-of-fact but sounded nervous. Concentrating on her, Troy nodded. "That's good."

She sat down and allowed her robe to slide open. "Left thigh today. Can't repeat injection sites too often. I probably seem calm, but I want you to know how I really feel."

She lifted one of her hands to him. "Touch my palm."

Troy did. It was damp, sweaty, and trembling slightly. He closed his hand around it.

She looked at their entwined hands for a long moment, then brought his to her mouth and kissed it. "Thanks," she whispered, then released his hand. "I really hate shots. Always have. When I was a little girl, I screamed every time I got a booster shot. So when the doctor told me I would be giving myself injections twice a day for the rest of my life, I asked about other options." She frowned in distaste. "None of them were good, so before I knew it, I was practicing on oranges. And then on me." She shot him a warning glance. "It's still not a dignified sight."

She swiped the alcohol pad across her thigh and hesitated for a few seconds. Her tension wrapped around his heart like a steel cord. Fear flashed through her eyes, and he wanted to hold her.

"God, I hate this," she whispered. She plunged the needle into her thigh. Her face wrinkled in a quick slice of pain. "Oh!" Two seconds passed, and she was tossing the syringe into the trash can.

She stood, took a deep breath, and smiled sheepishly. "All done."

Troy stood more slowly. "Why'd you finally let me see?"

"Because you asked," she told him, her eyes growing suspiciously shiny. "I've never had anyone love me the way you did." She swallowed and seemed to work at keeping her composure. Her voice was unsteady. "Enough to make me love him back. And I guess I wanted you to know that whatever you ask of me, even if it's hard, I'll try to give it to you." She met his gaze, her eyes awash with fear and love.

Troy's heart was so full, he couldn't speak. She loved him.

She bit her lip. "I'm getting very nervous, Troy. I just spilled my guts, and you're not saying anything."

Swearing, he still couldn't form words, so he lifted her in his arms and carried her to the bed. He set her down and followed after her.

"You're still not talk—"

He covered her mouth with his hand. "Give me a minute. I feel like Lazarus coming back from the dead. The last two weeks have been hell."

She lifted her hands to his face and looked at him in wonder. "I missed you. I hadn't counted on it, and it really annoyed me."

Troy felt a rusty chuckle bubble up from his chest. "Annoyed you enough to make you come to Tennessee so I could annoy you some more."

She smiled. "Yes."

He thought about how she'd finally let him watch her give herself an injection. It was crazy, but sharing that moment of vulnerability with her had felt almost as intimate as making love. He pushed open her robe and lowered his head to press a kiss to her thigh. He felt her fingers thread through his hair, and he closed his eyes for just a second.

"You said you'd give me anything I asked for," he said, looking up at her.

She met his gaze straight on. "Yes."

"I want to know all your secrets."

Her eyes widened. "Okay. But I might not know all of them myself."

"That's okay," he told her, feeling his gut tighten again. "I want your body next to mine every night and every morning."

She stared at him. "Yes."

He stared back at her, his heart hammering against his rib cage. "I can't get enough of you. Can't get close enough. I want you so much, it scares the hell out of me."

Her eyes filled with tears again. "I feel the same way, Troy. All you have to do is ask."

"I want to belong to you. I want you to belong to me."

She nodded, and he couldn't believe it.

"I want you to marry me."

"Yes," she said without hesitation.

He'd expected a long pause, an I'll-think-about-it, or a thank-you-but—"Again," he said, because his heart and his ears could hardly take it in. "Again."

"Yes," she said, and pulled his mouth to hers. "Yes, yes, yes," she whispered, punctuating each affirmation with a kiss. And after she demonstrated her yes for an hour, Troy finally began to believe.

EPILOGUE

"You look a little overwhelmed," Troy said to Senada as they stole a quick break from the guests at their wedding reception. The outdoor celebration was held on the lush, well-manicured grounds of a Chattanooga hotel. The late August afternoon was warm, and the lawn was overrun with Pendletons of every size and age.

Sin looked at Troy in amused irritation. She'd thought she'd hidden her emotions well, but it seemed Troy could always tell. "I'm integrating," she corrected.

He grinned. "You're wondering what the hell you've gotten into."

She slid him a suggestive look. "I'm hoping you're going to show me what I've gotten into."

His eyes darkened at her invitation. "You really don't want my brothers ribbing us for the next half century because we couldn't keep our hands off each other until the cake was served."

She shrugged. God, she loved to tease him. "Guess it depends on if you're better than cake."

"Let's dance," he said tersely, and dragged her onto the dance floor. A string trio played old standards. Adults and children alike danced to the easy music.

Sin spotted her father and waved at him. "Daddy thinks I've married into a family of hooligans."

"You have."

"Are you saying I should reconsider?"

He tightened his grip on her waist. "Too late."

Troy's brother Garth sidled up beside them with his wife, Erin. She was small and blond and Garth rarely left her side. He was the one they called the Pendleton Devil, and Senada saw a glint of it in his eyes every now and then. For the most part, though, he looked happy. "I think our brother-in-law Russ wants to make an announcement," Garth said.

Troy lifted an eyebrow. "Something about Carly?" he asked, referring to their sister.

Garth nodded. "I hear she's been hugging the toilet."

"Must be in the water," Troy muttered, tilting his head toward Nathan and his bride of two weeks, who was scheduled to deliver their baby within a month. "That means everyone but

Ethan and me has added to the world popula-
tion."

Sin stiffened slightly.

Troy squeezed her waist. "Don't worry,
honey. I want you all to myself for a while."

"I didn't say a word," she told him.

Troy grinned. "You didn't have to."

"Shut up and dance with your bride."

His eyes grew solemn. "My pleasure."

Sin's heart turned over as he pulled her
closer. Out of the corner of her eye, she saw
Troy's other brothers. The oldest, Daniel, was
holding his little girl in one hand and stealing a
kiss from his wife, Sara, at the same time. Ethan
and his new wife were wrapped around each
other. Jarod snatched peanuts from Augusta and
was teasing her to take a bite.

Senada smiled. "There's a whole lot of love
in this family. All the Pendleton men are taken. I
guess the Ladies Club can rest easy now," she
murmured, enjoying the closeness with Troy.
Being with him had changed her. She was more
open about her feelings because she knew she
could trust him to be there for her always. What
a feeling, she thought. What an incredible feeling. She pressed a kiss to his neck.

It was natural for him to turn to her, to take
her mouth, natural for a little caress to turn into
something more passionate. He broke away reluctantly, and she could feel his body begin to
respond. Hers did too.

"My, my," she said. "I do believe you are better than cake, Troy."

He swore under his breath. "When you look at me like that, I want to carry you up to our room and say to hell with the rest of this."

"Promises, promises," she whispered wickedly.

She watched in amazement as his self-restraint shredded right before her eyes. He picked her up in his arms and swept her past the punch bowl toward the back of the hotel.

"Troy!" The amused, surprised faces of their guests blurred together. Distantly, she heard gasps and laughter.

"It's your fault. You can push a man but so far. You gotta learn, Sin. There will be consequences to kissing me like that in public, dancing real close, and scorching me with one of your come-and-get-me looks."

He carried her through the lobby to the elevator. "Does this mean you want me to stop?"

"Hell no," he said, punching the button for their floor.

Her heart was pounding and melting at the same time. He looked so irritated and determined at the same time. She took a quick breath. "You mentioned consequences," she prompted.

He strode from the elevator toward their suite. "That's easy," he said. "I'm gonna love you till the only word you can say to me is yes."

"Oh, not that," she murmured, feigning horror.

He kicked the bedroom door shut behind them and allowed her body to slide down his, his mouth making love to hers. "Yes," he said.

Her brain went fuzzy. "Hmmmm."

"Yes," he prompted again.

"Yes," she whispered. And Senada fought tears, because she knew she'd spend a lifetime showing this man, this wonderful man, that her yes was forever.

THE EDITORS' CORNER

Summer must eventually come to an end, but romance never has to. In fact, next month LOVE-SWEPT brings you a heat wave of exciting, passionate tales that are just perfect for warding off the end-of-the-summer blues. Keep that iced drink handy!

Fayrene Preston's acclaimed DAMARON MARK series continues with **THE DAMARON MARK: THE SINNER,** LOVESWEPT #798. Sinclair Damaron hates himself for inspiring the fear that darkens Jillian Wythe's gray eyes as he lures her into his trap. Then Jillian awakens in a world of tropical beauty and is shocked to discover she wants Sin as much as her freedom! But a fever of revenge has the entire Damaron clan in its grip, and Jillian learns that Sin intends to use her as bait. An explosive story of danger and desire, dark sensuality and reckless romance—from #1 bestselling author Fayrene Preston.

Attraction sizzles on every page as Laura Taylor blends heartbreaking emotion and risky passion in **FALLEN ANGEL,** LOVESWEPT #799. When Thomas Coltrane's new next-door neighbor insists she wants him to keep his distance, he can't agree less. From her husky voice to her expressive hands that speak in sign language, Geneva Talmadge is one tantalizing challenge he's never faced before—in a courtroom or a bedroom. And he isn't about to let a little thing like her cool treatment of him stop him from winning her love. Award winner Laura Taylor has created a one-of-a-kind courtship that makes for nonstop reading.

Please welcome talented newcomer RaeAnne Thayne and her wildly romantic debut, **THE MATING GAME,** LOVESWEPT #800. Chase Samuelson is still the most gorgeous male Carly Jacobs has ever known. She's never forgotten her teenage crush on him or his betrayal years before, but now he's back and the chemistry between them is more combustible than ever. She'd given Chase her heart, trusted him with her dreams. Is his return her second chance to taste the fire of his kiss? Chase and Carly's bittersweet reunion is part genuinely touching, part brashly funny—and 100 percent wonderful. Look for more RaeAnne Thayne novels in the months to come.

Fresh from her triumphant THE THREE MUSKETEERS trilogy, Donna Kauffman now takes us on a journey through Cajun mysteries with **BAYOU HEAT,** LOVESWEPT #801. Though naked and bloodied in her bathtub, Teague Comeaux gives Dr. Erin McClure a smile wicked enough to charm a lady out of her clothes! She'd asked for a guide into voodoo country, but Teague looks like trouble. And when he escorts her right into the middle of danger and intrigue, she's certain he's the devil in disguise. Donna Kauffman weaves dark seduction into every page of this steamy, spellbinding romance.

Happy reading!

With warmest wishes,

Beth de Guzman   Shauna Summers
Senior Editor   Editor

P.S. Watch for these Bantam women's fiction titles coming next month: Rising star Susan Krinard returns to the land of the bestselling PRINCE OF WOLVES with **PRINCE OF SHADOWS**. And in **WALKING RAIN**, Susan Wade makes a stunning debut that showcases her disarmingly original style and deft supernatural touches. And immediately following this page, preview the Bantam women's fiction titles on sale *now*!

Treat yourself to

MISCHIEF

the newest hardcover by *New York Times*
bestselling author

Amanda Quick

*To help her foil a ruthless fortune hunter, Imogen
Waterstone needs a man.
Not just any man, but Matthias Marshall,
the intrepid explorer known as
"Coldblooded Colchester."*

"You pass yourself off as a man of action, but
now it seems that you are not that sort of man at
all," Imogen told Matthias.

"I do not pass myself off as anything but
what I am, you exasperating little—"

"Apparently you write fiction rather than
fact, sir. Bad enough that I thought you to be a
clever, resourceful gentleman given to feats of
daring. I have also been laboring under the
equally mistaken assumption that you are a man
who would put matters of honor ahead of petty
considerations of inconvenience."

"Are you calling my honor as well as my
manhood into question?"

"Why shouldn't I? You are clearly indebted

to me, sir, yet you obviously wish to avoid making payment on that debt."

"I was indebted to your uncle, not to you."

"I have explained to you that I inherited the debt," she retorted.

Matthias took another gliding step into the grim chamber. "Miss Waterstone, you try my patience."

"I would not dream of doing so," she said, her voice dangerously sweet. "I have concluded that you will not do at all as an associate in my scheme. I hereby release you from your promise. Begone, sir."

"Bloody hell, woman. You are not going to get rid of me so easily." Matthias crossed the remaining distance between them with two long strides and clamped his hands around her shoulders.

Touching her was a mistake. Anger metamorphosed into desire in the wink of an eye.

For an instant he could not move. His insides seemed to have been seized by a powerful fist. Matthias tried to breathe, but Imogen's scent filled his head, clouding his brain. He looked down into the bottomless depths of her blue-green eyes and wondered if he would drown. He opened his mouth to conclude the argument with a suitably repressive remark, but the words died in his throat.

The outrage vanished from Imogen's gaze. It was replaced by sudden concern. "My lord? Is something wrong?"

"Yes." It was all he could do to get the word past his teeth.

"What is it?" She began to look alarmed. "Are you ill?"

"Quite possibly."

"Good heavens. I had not realized. That no doubt explains your odd behavior."

"No doubt."

"Would you care to lie down on the bed for a few minutes?"

"I do not think that would be a wise move at this juncture." She was so soft. He could feel the warmth of her skin through the sleeves of her prim, practical gown. He realized that he longed to discover if she made love with the same impassioned spirit she displayed in an argument. He forced himself to remove his hands from her shoulders. "We had best finish this discussion at some other time."

"Nonsense," she said bracingly. "I do not believe in putting matters off, my lord."

Matthias shut his eyes for the space of two or three seconds and took a deep breath. When he lifted his lashes he saw that Imogen was watching him with a fascinated expression. "Miss Waterstone," he began with grim determination. "I am trying to employ reason here."

"You're going to help me, aren't you?" She started to smile.

"I beg your pardon?"

"You've changed your mind, haven't you? Your sense of honor has won out." Her eyes glowed. "Thank you, my lord. I knew you would assist me in my plans." She gave him an approving little pat on the arm. "And you must not concern yourself with the other matter."

"What other matter?"

"Why, your lack of direct experience with bold feats and daring adventure. I quite understand. You need not be embarrassed by the fact that you are not a man of action, sir."

"Miss Waterstone—"

"Not everyone can be an intrepid sort, after all," she continued blithely. "You need have no fear. If anything dangerous occurs in the course of my scheme, I shall deal with it."

"The very thought of you taking charge of a dangerous situation is enough to freeze the marrow in my bones."

"Obviously you suffer from a certain weakness of the nerves. But we shall contrive to muddle through. Try not to succumb to the terrors of the imagination, my lord. I know you must be extremely anxious about what lies ahead, but I assure you, I will be at your side every step of the way."

"Will you, indeed?" He felt dazed.

"I shall protect you." Without any warning, Imogen put her arms around him and gave him what was no doubt meant to be a quick, reassuring hug.

The tattered leash Matthias was using to hold on to his self-control snapped. Before Imogen could pull away, he wrapped her close.

"Sir?" Her eyes widened with surprise.

"The only aspect of this situation that truly alarms me, Miss Waterstone," he said roughly, "is the question of who will protect me from you?"

RAVEN AND THE COWBOY
by Sandra Chastain

"An extremely talented author whose writing
is . . . warm and real and lovely."
—*New York Times* bestselling author
Heather Graham

*He first came to her in a dream: a sleek and tawny
cougar with the power to protect her. So when Raven
Alexander awoke to find herself lying beside the rugged stranger, she wasn't afraid. He might be an un-
ruly cowboy with a checkered past but Raven believed
the spirit guides had sent him to help her find the
sacred Arapaho treasure.*

It was the sound of thunder that woke Tucker,
followed by hard, pelting rain that stung his face.
He sat up, disoriented for a moment as he tried
to remember where he was.

Rain. He was outside. But where was Yank? A
flash of lightning lit up the sky, revealing the side
of the cliff and an opening in the rock before
him. He pushed himself onto his elbows, his head
vibrating as if he'd been hit by the lightning
flashing in the distance.

Gingerly he began to feel his way toward the
wall, his hand encountering something in the

darkness—something that ought not to be there. An ankle. A slim ankle leading to a foot encased in a soft moccasin.

Tucker froze. He wasn't alone. Wherever on the west side of hell he was, he had a woman with him. But why wasn't she having a reaction to his touch? Another jagged streak of silver split the sky and illuminated her face—he could see that she was an Indian, wearing a buckskin dress.

He must have had more to drink than he'd thought. Maybe he was hallucinating. Or this was a dream. No, the leg he held was real. It was warm and soft and feminine. But something was wrong. No woman would sleep through a storm.

The rain came down harder. If he didn't get the woman out of this downpour, she'd get sick. Taking her by the arm, he tugged her against him. With one hand behind him and the other arm around her waist, he inched away from the edge.

At last, with one final jerk, they were inside the cave, out of the elements. Tucker shivered from being wet. His bedroll was on Yank's back, wherever Yank was. Tucker didn't want to think that the horse had gone over the edge with him. Tucker always took care of his horse. Just like his namesakes, the big black was indestructible. They were a good match, a Southern Rebel and a horse named Yank. Both were survivors.

The cave was small and damp. The woman, still lying against his chest, was cold. He shook her gently, waiting for a reaction. But the only response he felt was his own as the top of his index finger found the space beneath her breast.

"Ma'am . . . Lady . . . I beg your pardon, but would you wake up."

She moaned and turned slightly so that her face was against his chest. His hand, below her breast only moments ago, was now holding it. Tucker froze, waiting for her to come to her senses and chastise him for his liberties.

But she didn't wake. He had the absurd feeling that he'd been cut into two people. His head ached fiercely while the lower half of his body, very much alert, announced a raging male hunger. Until he understood what was happening, he'd forced his thoughts and touch away from that need as he cradled her head and laid her down.

That's when he found it, the wound, blood now dried across a deep cut in her scalp behind her ear. However she'd come to join him in this godforsaken place, she, too had come accidentally. Nobody deliberately fell off a cliff. But what was he going to do? The rain hadn't let up. It was too dark to see how to get back to the trail, and he wasn't sure he was steady enough on his feet to get them there.

If he could find some dry sticks or limbs, he could build a fire. Reluctantly he let go of her and waited for the next flash of lightning. Once he was reasonably certain that they weren't sharing the cave with any animals, he began to explore, encountering the remains of a pack rat's nest.

In the cantina he'd had tobacco and matches.

He reached into his shirt pocket, hoping they were still there. They were, along with the half-breed's gold nuggets and the watch fob. Now the bandits had another excuse for chasing him—the loot.

Shielding his meager makings of a fire from the wind, Tucker cupped his hands and struck the first match against a stone. It flared briefly, then died. There were only a few matches left. He couldn't afford to waste another.

Closing his eyes, he prayed for a moment of calm as he lit another match. This time the moss blazed up, igniting the sticks. Momentarily he had a tiny fire going.

Though meager, the fire soon warmed the air inside the small cave. Tucker sluiced water through the woman's head wound and winced at the depth of it. He didn't know why she wasn't dead. She could die still if he didn't get her warm.

Removing his sheepskin jacket, he covered her, checking beneath her wet clothing for a sign that her body temperature was rising. It wasn't. Finally, because he knew nothing else to do, he lay down beside her and pulled her against him. He didn't intend to doze off, but the heat from the fire and the woman's body soon made him drowsy.

As the storm raged outside, Tucker Farrell covered himself and the woman with his jacket. Then he did something he had never done with a woman before. He slept.

She cast a spell of passion in a
dangerous duel of hearts.

From the dazzling new talent of
Juliana Garnett
author of *The Quest*
comes a spellbinding romantic tale
for those who believe in

THE MAGIC

*Although Rhys ap Griffyn hurried back from King
Richard's crusade to claim his heritage, he met his fate
in a forest clearing, in a mysterious woman who
barred his way and set his blood afire. Wrapped in
shadows, the lady with raven-dark hair might have
been an enchanted creature, for the locals had warned
him not to ride on Beltane Eve. But Rhys didn't believe in faeries, and the exotic Sasha felt real enough
to him. . . .*

He had done no more than press his lips to
the dimple at the corner of her mouth when Rhys
heard a voice callling his name, faraway and insistent. He tried to ignore it, but the persistent
sound grew too near. Halting, he looked up with
a scowl at the interruption. It took a moment for
his surroundings to come fully into focus, then
he saw with some surprise that he was far from

the wooded pool where he'd first met her. An alder sheltered them beneath its branches, and a small burn trickled merrily by, water splashing over the rocks. A grassy meadow sloped downward from the trees.

She shifted, then laid her fingers against his cheek; her eyes glowed softly when he glanced back down at her. "I must go," she murmured. "It grows late."

He caught her hand, holding it. "Nay, wait. 'Tis only Brian. I'll send him away."

She slowly withdrew her hand and rose to her feet, and he followed reluctantly. "I cannot . . ." She cast a glance over her shoulder as Brian's voice grew louder and nearer. Gathering her cloak around her, she took a step away from him, repeating, "I must go."

He grabbed her hand again, fingers digging into her tender skin with shameless urgency. "Wait. Tell me your name and where you reside. We'll meet again once I send Brian away."

Her smile deepened as she removed her hand from his clasp and took a backward step. "Yea, we shall meet again."

He started to reach for her anew, determined not to let her go so easily, but Brian's voice made him pause. "Rhys!" came the strident call, followed by pained yowls that dwindled into rough curses directed at a clump of brambles.

Curse Brian. He glanced away, and shouted impatiently that he would be there in a moment. When he turned back, the maid was gone. Jésu— she'd been there one moment, standing near the crowded branches of flowering hawthorns, but now she was not to be seen. He looked around, dumbfounded and furious.

"Rhys," came Brian's voice again, sounding relieved and breathless as he crashed toward him through a raspberry patch. "Where have you been all day?"

"All day?" Rhys dragged his gaze away from the spot where the maid had last stood and spun to face his knight. " 'Tis but early morn. What's the matter with you? Did you not mark that I was occupied—?"

The snarled oath that accompanied this demand made Brian swallow hard. "Yea, lord," he said, looking down, "I marked it well, yet—"

"Yet you chose to ignore it." He shook his head irritably. "Now she has fled, and God only knows if I'll ever see her again."

"She?" Brian looked up from plucking a thorn from his arm, blinking rapidly. "You were with a woman, my lord?"

"Did you not say you marked it well? By all the saints, Brian, I begin to think you wine-mazed."

"Nay, lord, I've been searching for you. We thought ill had befallen you when we couldn't find you."

Rhys jerked at the ties of his loosened chausses. Damn the ache. "I went to bathe at the pond—" He broke off suddenly and looked up. "My armor and helm. I must have left them off, but I don't remember. . . ."

Brian was looking at him strangely, and Rhys

narrowed his eyes. "Why do you look at me like that?"

"We found your armor and helmet by the pool earlier." Brian swallowed heavily. " 'Tis near midday, and we despaired of finding you— you've been with her, haven't you? The Elf Queen?"

*To enter the sweepstakes outlined below, you must respond by the date specified and
follow all entry instructions published elsewhere in this offer.*

DREAM COME TRUE SWEEPSTAKES

Sweepstakes begins 9/1/94, ends 1/15/96. To qualify for the Early Bird Prize, entry must be received by the date specified elsewhere in this offer. Winners will be selected in random drawings on 2/29/96 by an independent judging organization whose decisions are final. Early Bird winner will be selected in a separate drawing from among all qualifying entries.

Odds of winning determined by total number of entries received. Distribution not to exceed 300 million.

Estimated maximum retail value of prizes: Grand (1) $25,000 (cash alternative $20,000); First (1) $2,000; Second (1) $750; Third (50) $75; Fourth (1,000) $50; Early Bird (1) $5,000. Total prize value: $86,500.

Automobile and travel trailer must be picked up at a local dealer; all other merchandise prizes will be shipped to winners. Awarding of any prize to a minor will require written permission of parent/guardian. If a trip prize is won by a minor, s/he must be accompanied by parent/legal guardian. Trip prizes subject to availability and must be completed within 12 months of date awarded. Blackout dates may apply. Early Bird trip is on a space available basis and does not include port charges, gratuities, optional shore excursions and onboard personal purchases. Prizes are not transferable or redeemable for cash except as specified. No substitution for prizes except as necessary due to unavailability. Travel trailer and/or automobile license and registration fees are winners' responsibility as are any other incidental expenses not specified herein.

Early Bird Prize may not be offered in some presentations of this sweepstakes. Grand through third prize winners will have the option of selecting any prize offered at level won. All prizes will be awarded. Drawing will be held at 204 Center Square Road, Bridgeport, NJ 08014. Winners need not be present. For winners list (available in June, 1996), send a self-addressed, stamped envelope by 1/15/96 to: Dream Come True Winners, P.O. Box 572, Gibbstown, NJ 08027.

THE FOLLOWING APPLIES TO THE SWEEPSTAKES ABOVE:

No purchase necessary. No photocopied or mechanically reproduced entries will be accepted. Not responsible for lost, late, misdirected, damaged, incomplete, illegible, or postage-die mail. Entries become the property of sponsors and will not be returned.

Winner(s) will be notified by mail. Winner(s) may be required to sign and return an affidavit of eligibility/release within 14 days of date on notification or an alternate may be selected. Except where prohibited by law, entry constitutes permission to use of winners' names, hometowns, and likenesses for publicity without additional compensation. Void where prohibited or restricted. All federal, state, provincial, and local laws and regulations apply.

All prize values are in U.S. currency. Presentation of prizes may vary; values at a given prize level will be approximately the same. All taxes are winners' responsibility.

Canadian residents, in order to win, must first correctly answer a time-limited skill testing question administered by mail. Any litigation regarding the conduct and awarding of a prize in this publicity contest by a resident of the province of Quebec may be submitted to the Regie des loteries et courses du Quebec.

Sweepstakes is open to legal residents of the U.S., Canada, and Europe (in those areas where made available) who have received this offer.

Sweepstakes in sponsored by Ventura Associates, 1211 Avenue of the Americas, New York, NY 10036 and presented by independent businesses. Employees of these, their advertising agencies and promotional companies involved in this promotion, and their immediate families, agents, successors, and assignees shall be ineligible to participate in the promotion and shall not be eligible for any prizes covered herein.   SWP 3/95